The Stolen Brand

D.W. Lewis

ISBN: 9781972803066
Renaissance Hands Books
2nd Edition

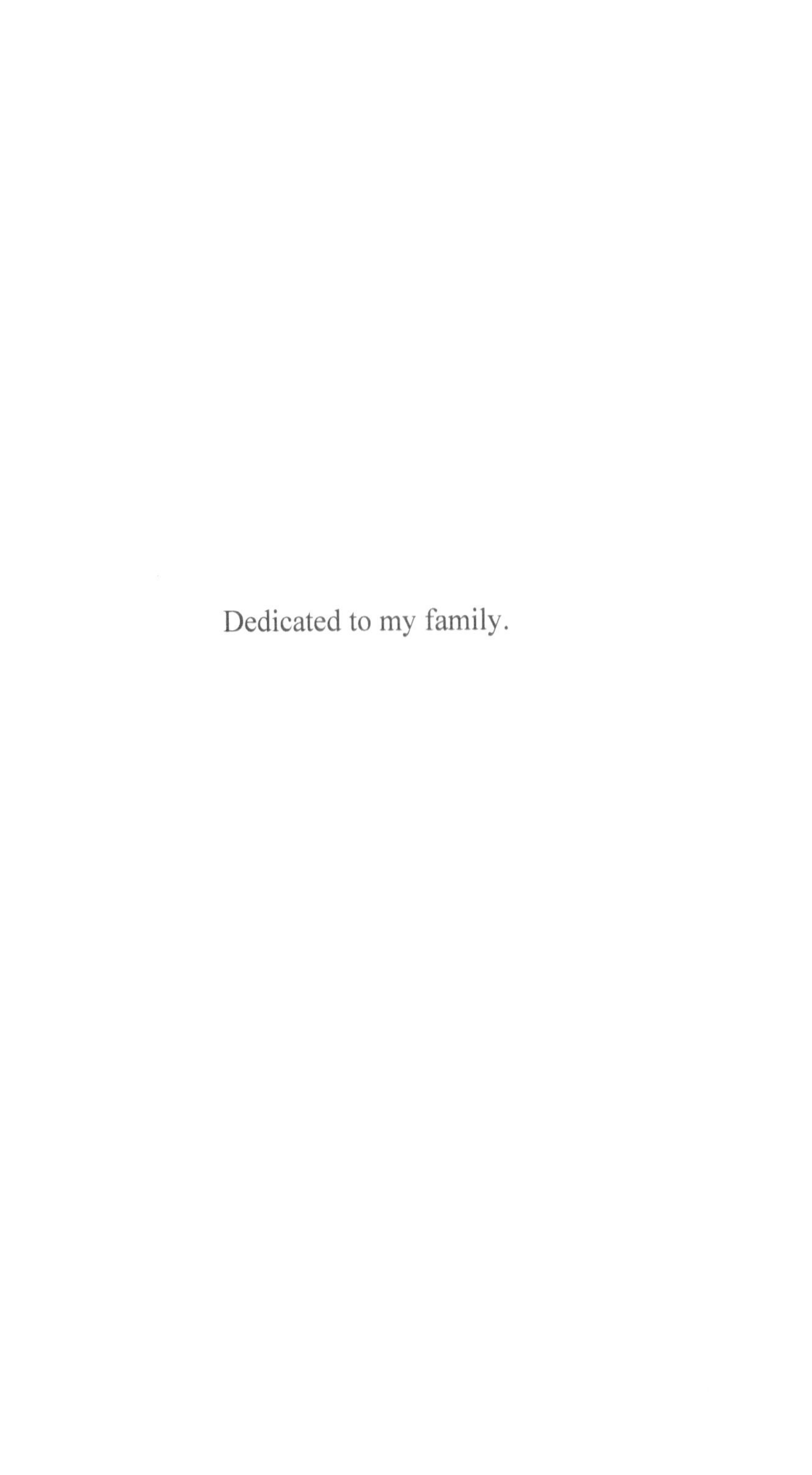

Dedicated to my family.

Chapter 1

The morning mist has just left the fields as I walk out of the stable. It is early spring, and the morning air still has a touch of a winter chill in it. I put my gloves on quickly before grabbing the lead rope I'm using to bring Little Red out of the stable. Red is a chestnut horse that my girl, Emily, had named for me. She is always fond of naming the animals. I had never really bothered to name horses before Emily came along, so it amuses me to call the horse Little Red. It is nice to have reminders of little Emily while on the trail. I chuckle at that thought, "little Emily," almost a woman now at thirteen.

I lead Little Red to the gate, close the stable and mount her. I have come a long way since I first came to Colorado, as a young buck looking to make a name for myself. I have done that, but not in the way I reckoned. Hard work and a bit of luck brought me to where I am now; owner of my own land and recently able to expand my ranch. As I headed out to the trail I see my oldest son, Cody, coming out of the trees. He rides over to me and smiles.

"Hey Pa." he says, "I thought I would ride with you to the new land." Cody looks more like his Ma than he does me, he has her golden hair and easy smile. He has my deep brown eyes and broad shoulders though. It is no wonder all the girls in town are angling to catch him.

We ride quietly together, enjoying the quiet of the trail in the morning. A few birds are starting to announce the arrival of spring and some of the other wildlife start to rustle around, probably looking for any food left after a long, cold winter. Cody and I ride along the pass and come to the fence that marked the old boundary to my land. Beyond the fence the land takes a turn towards the sky as the slope of the mountains makes a sudden increase. I got the land cheap because it really isn't good for much. The previous owner mined all the gold, and it was now worthless to him; he was glad to let it go.

I lead Cody to a trailhead and the two of us ride single file up into the mountains. The trail is very narrow, but we take it to where I know there lies the one redeeming feature of this land. The hills on both sides of us open up and suddenly we are in a valley. The valley isn't very big, about 30 acres, but it is well hidden. I wouldn't have known it was here if it weren't for the fact that years ago, I was looking for a stray and the trail led me here. There is a small creek that runs across the small valley floor, and there is little vegetation. As we arrive in the valley, we startle a family of deer that are drinking at the creek.

"It's perfect" Cody says.

"It is, I came up here last winter and it's well sheltered," I tell him. "We might be able to keep some of the smaller cows up here during the winter, keep them out of the cold."

"That's good," Cody says looking around, "this trail the only way in?"

"As far as I know" I answer.

"Then this will be perfect." Cody says with a smile. I'm so proud of the expertise he's starting to show. He has been raised around cattle, so it all comes so naturally to him. Sometimes I regret my upbringing that made it so difficult when I started working with cattle, I recon it's only right for a father to give his children things he didn't have growing up. Cody turns his horse back toward the trail and looks over at me. "I'm going to check on Jesse and the hands." Jesse's my other boy, at just seventeen he loves to be out with the cattle and helping out.

Jesse heads out of the valley and I take another minute to ride around the valley to make sure there isn't another way in or out of here. As I'm making my way back to what I have confirmed is the only entrance I catch movement out of the corner of my eye. I look up the slope to where I swear I can see something. I can just see the outline of a man on a horse moving further along the edge of a drop off into the valley. Before I can make out any other details he's gone. I'm not sure who would be watching from up there, so I look for a path up there. By the time I get up, there is nobody around. I look around and find some signs of a camp. Probably just someone passing through.
I decide to head back to the house and check on Emily and Jane before heading out to the

fields. Jane and I have been married for twenty-four years now. It still gets me that a woman as beautiful as her would want to settle down with an old cowhand like me. Her long golden hair is now speckled with grey, and she might have put on a little weight since we were married, but she is just as beautiful to me as the day we met. I was working for her Pa, punching cows, when we first met. Her Pa was the one that helped me get started with this place, selling me my first twenty head of cattle for well under what they were worth. He told me to make sure his grandchildren grew up right, without wanting for anything. I took that to heart.

As I approach the stable, I look at my homestead that I had slowly built up over the years. What had started as a one-room cabin now had three bedrooms, a sitting room, and a nice kitchen with a cast iron stove that was worth the cost to make Jane happy. Last summer the boys and I added to the porch out front so Jane and I could sit out there on a cool evening and relax. We haven't really had much chance to do that as we are always working, but I suppose a day will come that we will.

Close to the house are a barn and stable, the stable also has a room at the back for our hands. We have made enough money in the last few years to hire ten cowboys to help run the ranch. Cody is a good leader and takes care of running the hands. I enjoy being out there with them, but as I get older my body doesn't always appreciate it. I ride up to the stable and dismount Little Red, I lead her into her stall before stripping off her saddle and blanket and giving her a quick rub-down. After putting some grain in a bucket for her I walk over to the house.

The front door of the house is open, and Emily is sweeping the sitting room. She smiles as she sees me walk up to the house. "Pa!" she exclaims, "how was the new land?"

"It looks good." I say, "where's your Ma?"

"The kitchen I think," she replies, "she's working on some bread for my boys." Emily calls all the hands "her boys" which rubs me the wrong way, that's probably why she does it. It must be hard to have a protective father and two protective brothers. Any boy that comes calling for Emily will have no easy task. There might be bias involved, but Emily is one of the most beautiful girls in the county, the proof lies in the number of boys that hang out around her whenever we go to town. She has golden hair, and is starting to develop some womanly curves, that her apron isn't doing a good enough job of hiding for my liking. In a few years she can start thinking of boys, but she's still a bit young.

I walk through the sitting room and past the dining room table that I made when Cody was very young in hopes of having a big family. The kitchen is a good size and has enough room for a smaller table for the girls to use for baking. Jane is in there kneading a big ball of white dough, she is most beautiful when she is making something in the kitchen. She loves to do things for the hands, either cooking, caring for them when sick or just spending time talking with them. She is mother hen to even the roughest cowboy. I suppose when she was young, she saw all the hands as "her boys" I think with a smile.

"Henry" she smiles up at me as I walk in, "Are you happy with the new purchase?"

I sit in a chair close to her, taking off my gloves thankful for the warm kitchen "I think it will be the perfect place for some of the older cows and maybe even some of the younger ones that won't be quite big enough to survive winter."

"That will be wonderful" Jane says, "how many did we lose last winter?" Jane goes over to the stove where there is a pot of coffee brewing and pours a cup of coffee that she then sits down across from me.

"At least thirty," I say thoughtfully, "which isn't too bad considering how bad the winter was. We have some good mountain cattle now, most of the weak ones have died off giving me a good breeding stock." I am very happy with how my cattle have done over the winter, we usually lose some of the herd over the winter but with every year we see fewer of them go. This left me with a herd that could handle the cold winters up at this elevation.

"Are you going to town this week?" Jane says, interrupting my thoughts.

"Yes," I answer. "I have to get some wire, we don't have a lot of fencing to do on the new land, but I would like to make sure the cows aren't able to stray from the valley."

"Good, I think Emily and I will come with you. We need some flour and sugar, and Emily is outgrowing her clothes, I need more fabric." I agree that this is a good idea. I finish my cup of coffee and then stand up.

"We'll go in tomorrow." I say as I get ready to go outside again, "the sooner we get that fencing up the better." As I stand up and turn around Emily walks through the door into the kitchen.

"Sherrif Kenedy is here to see you," she tells me. "He's in the sitting room." "Thanks" I tell Emily. "Could you bring us some coffee?"

"I already asked, he said he was in a hurry. Said he didn't want any." Emily walks over to the door we put into the back of the kitchen to give easy access to the pump out back. On her way she grabs the mop bucket. I walk out of the kitchen and see Buck Kenedy sitting in one of our new high back chairs that Jane and I had bought each other for Christmas. They were those fancy ones with padded seats. Kenedy looked at me with a wry smile on his face.

"You're getting pretty fancy out here," he said with a smile.

"Getting comfortable is more like it," I shot back sitting in the other high back chair. "Had a pretty good year last year and decided to treat ourselves."

"Well don't let Annie see these or she'll be wanting one herself."

"So," I ask leaning forward in my chair, "what brings you out here?"

The sheriff leaned forward as well, "I'm afraid there's a bit of trouble in town." The town was peaceful since Kenedy took over as sheriff; he was strict on the rules of the town. I voted for him myself. He is a big man, stands a good six inches about my six foot three, always clean shaven and hair closely shorn. I wasn't sure what kind of trouble could bring him to me. "There's a new outfit in town that has been talking up how they have bought everything from the Platte River over to Morrison's Pass."

"That's a lot of territory," I say, starting to realize where this was going,

Morrison's Pass went along some of my fence line. "I guess they're new neighbors."

"Yeah," Kenedy continued, "didn't you buy that old prospector's claim? Because that's in that territory he's talking about."

"Well, maybe he's talking about that," I say thoughtfully. "Maybe not. Maybe he's just got a few things mixed up."

"He sounds pretty sure of himself" says Kenedy. I lean back into my chair and start to fish out my tobacco pouch from my pocket. Sometimes when a man needs a minute to think, rolling a cigarette gives his hands something to do. I roll a cigarette and then pull out a match to light it, after I get it going, I look at Kenedy again.

"I just filed the paperwork in the land office last week, it's all legal." I say with confidence, "If there is any question it can easily be answered." This answer seems to make Kenedy happy. He stands up and so do I, we walk to the door and he offers his hand.

"I'm glad to hear you have your paperwork in order," he says as we shake hands, "makes my job a lot easier." I watch as Kenedy walks out to his horse. I walk back to the kitchen and Jane is getting the dough she was kneading into a big bowl to let it rest.

"What was that about?" she asks once she sees me.

"Apparently someone is telling people in town that they bought the old Miller place" I said, "I'm sure it's nothing serious." Jane nods and goes back to what she is working on. "When we are in town tomorrow, I will ask around and see if anyone has any information on this new outfit." The nice thing about Victor is that it is a small town and anyone who moves to the area tends to get noticed. I walk around the table and kiss Jane on the head before heading out the kitchen door, past where Emily is filling the mop bucket.

"We're going to town tomorrow," I say to her. She looks up at me and smiles.

"Can I ride Boots?" she asks. Boots is the name she has given a young paint we just acquired.

"Good plan," I say, I'll tell your brothers to saddle her up fist thing.

Chapter 2

The town of Victor, Colorado popped up shortly after gold was found in the mountains. At one point there were hundreds of miners living in tents all around the town, but over the years the gold was all mined out and it dwindled down to a general store, a couple of saloons and a few other buildings. If it weren't for the fact that it is halfway between Boulder and Canon City, I don't think it would have survived at all. As I ride into town on my wagon, Jane by my side and Emily riding beside us on Boots, I look around at all the familiar faces. So many people I've known for years and very few new faces in the crowd. We stop in front of the general store and walk in. Adam Briggs, the store's owner, is out on the front step, posting a bill advertising what has come in on the last shipment of goods. "Mornin' Adam" I say as I step off the wagon, tying the horses to the post out front of the store, "how's business."

"Can't complain" says Adam as he walks over to shake my hand. Adam is a tall man and almost as broad as he is tall. He almost always wears his bowler hat to cover up his balding head. “Just got a new shipment of fabrics from New York” he says to Jane as she walks up to us.

“Perfect,” says Jane, “we’ll be needing to make some new dresses for Emily.”

“I got some premade dresses in too, some really pretty ones too by my wife’s reckoning” he says with a smile. I walk into the store to let him talk about fabric and dresses with my ladies. Adam’s wife Evelyn is standing behind the counter, looking over a ledger as I come in. Adam and the girls follow him as he leads them over to the fabric and then leaves them to look at everything and comes back over to me. “Is there anything you need?” he asks me.

“Just some fencing wire,” I say, “need to put some fences up on my new land.”

“New land?” he asks.

“Yes, bought out John Miller last week,” I say. He gives me a confused look and then walks over behind the counter. He then looks down at a scrap of paper he has behind the counter.

"John Miller?" he murmurs "well I thought that was part of the new Lazy K outfit."

"Never heard of the Lazy K" I say.

"Yeah," he nods "new in town. Just came in yesterday for supplies. Big company by the looks of it, brought in a few hundred head of cattle."

"Kenedy told me they bought a big parcel of land."

"Yes. I heard that they also bought the old Miller place."

"Sheriff Kenedy heard the same thing." I guess I'm needing to talk to the owner of the Lazy K. "I have a bill of sale for the old Miller place, but it makes sense people think they bought it. They bought up a lot of land."

"Fortunately for me, they also need to supply their whole outfit." Adam says with a smile. "Anyway, how much wire do you need?" I tell him and he shuffles off to fill my order. I look over at Jane and Emily, who have now been joined by Evelyn and are fawning over fabrics and some premade dresses. I imagine this is going to end up being an expensive trip to town. I look outside and across the street at the saloon there are a few horses with brands I don't recognize. I decide to walk over there and see if I can straighten things out. I let Jane and Emily know I'll be back soon and walk over to the saloon.

I'm not big on saloons anymore, settling down will do that to you, but I still will stop in for a drink and to catch up on local news. As I walk in, I see Lou is working the bar, Lou is getting up in age, having been in town since the founding. He looks over as I walk in and gives me a nod. I know most of the people here today, but there are three strangers sitting at a table over in the corner. I walk over to the table and take in the men, they are all dressed for the trail, one of them was wearing two guns with the holsters tied down. I figured him for the most dangerous as he likely fancied himself a gunfighter. Maybe he was good, but I wasn't about to go trying to find out.

"Gentlemen," I start off, "are you working for the Lazy K?"

"That's right," says the gunfighter "who are you?"

“My name is Henry Locke” I say, “owner of the Rocking A ranch, I was wondering if you could put me in touch with your boss.”

“What for?” the gunfighter again. He looks at me with suspicion.

“Just want to talk business,” I reply, “I hear we are neighbors.”

“He’s up at camp, it’s..” starts another of the men before the gunfighter gives him a look.

“Yeah” the gunfighter interrupts, “we’ll tell him you're looking for him.”

“Thanks” I say to the men. “Our house is set back off of Pike’s pass, about a mile from where the creek meets the river, he’s welcome to drop by anytime.” I turn away from the men and walk over to the bar. Lou’s been watching me this whole time and gives me a wary look as I walk over to him. He pulls out a beer bottle, which is what I normally drink when at the saloon and hands it to me.

“Thanks Lou,” I say taking a sip from the beer.

“What was you talking to them boys about?” asks Lou.

"They work for my new neighbor," I tell him.

"That one with the guns tied low is lookin' for trouble," Lou tells me. I look at Lou and take another drink of my beer.

"What makes you think that?" I ask.

"He's picked a few fights, tryin' to get someone to draw on him." I look back at the three men, who are now talking quietly among themselves, it looks like they are arguing. One of the men quickly stands and heads out to his horse, the gunfighter walks over to the bar, leaving the last one by himself at the table. The gunfighter looks like he's sizing me up.

"Help you?" Lou asks the gunfighter.

"Whiskey" says the man, still looking at me. You can tell he's trying to look tough, he's young, maybe twenty-four, and stands a bit shorter than average. He strikes me as the kind of man that thinks he's tougher than he is. I ignore him and look over to the man left at the table, he's older and looks confident in who he is. He's trying hard to ignore me, but I can see he has also unholstered his gun and it is sitting discreetly on his lap. I look back over to the gunfighter.

"Look," I say to him "I just want to talk to your boss. We don't need any trouble."

"My boss is a private person," says the gunfighter.

"That is fine by me" I say, "I'm good to meet him anywhere."

"Say he doesn't want to meet," says the gunfighter.

"That's his prerogative," I say with a smile, "just being neighborly."

"His what?" asks the man.

"Prerogative" I say, "that means his choice."

"You think you're so smart? Using them big words?" his hand is starting to twitch by his gun. I take a long drag from my beer, looking cool on the outside even though every nerve is on edge. Lou looks from the gunfighter to me.

"Lassiter" Lou says, "best be careful. Locke is a good hand with a gun."

"Maybe he was" says the gunfighter, Lassiter, "he's an old man now." Lou was right, this man was looking for a fight. Now

I'm not opposed to using a gun to shut a man up, would be hypocritical of me to have that opinion, but I'm also tired of just giving in to every idiot wanting to prove themselves. I decided I had enough of this, so I act quickly.

"Old?" I say as I let a right hook fly. This took Lassiter by surprise as it connected with his jaw and knocked him back into the stool behind him. He tripped over his own feet and ended up sprawling on the floor. Before he can get his feet under him, I take a step toward him, towering over him. I grew up with three brothers, and every Sunday afternoon was for bare knuckle fighting, a tradition I kept up with my boys. My first punch was enough to ring anyone's bell, and you could see this man Lassiter is struggling to get back up. I look over at his friend at the table and see he is starting to raise his pistol, so I quickly draw mine and point it at him. Now I'm not as fast as some of those gunfighters in the dime novels that my boys like to read, but I'm still quick. Fast enough to take the fellow by surprise. He quickly re-holstered his gun.

"We good?" I ask him.

"We're good" he responds. I turn my attention back to Lassiter who is finally getting back to his senses. As he comes up, I can see his hand go towards his gun, so with my right foot, I catch his hand and bring my foot up throwing him off balance again. My gun is still in my hand, so I turn it on him and look him in the eye.

"I still don't want any trouble" I tell him, "maybe don't make any." Lassiter quietly sits back down on the ground with his hands raised up in surrender. Lou looks over the bar down at the man with a big smile.

"I told you," he says, "Locke here is something of a local legend."

"Very local," I say with a smile as I put my Colt away. I look back down at Lassiter and then offer him a hand to help him up. He accepts the help and then pushes my hand away as soon as he is upright again. He is obviously embarrassed that I managed to get the upper hand. Lassiter walks back over to this friend and tells him they are heading out. His friend shrugs and follows him out the door.

"That was fun" Lou says with a smile.

"Not for me," I say rubbing my knuckles, "I haven't hit someone that hard in a while, it's not as easy on the hand as it used to be." Lou laughs and offers me another beer, which I refuse before taking my leave and heading back to the general store.

Jane is standing out by the wagon as I come out of the saloon. She looks at me rubbing my knuckles and she gets a disappointed look on her face. I walk over to her and give her a quick hug.

"What happened?" she asks me "I just saw two men rush out of that saloon like it was on fire."

"Just a couple of cowboys looking for trouble," I tell her. "I told them my Mrs. doesn't approve of fighting, and they should go home."

She looks at me, obviously not believing me but decides to let it go. Emily walks out of the store, carrying several packages. "How expensive was this trip to the store?" I ask Jane.

"I don't think we need to worry about that," says Jane with a smile, "we've both had our fun." As she laughs at her own joke, I go help Emily get her load into the wagon. Adam has brought the fencing material I needed out from his warehouse behind the store and comes out to help me load it into the wagon.

As we are headed home, Jane looks at me again, "what did happen in that saloon?" she asks.

"I tried making an appointment with the owner of the Lazy K, but his hands thought they would rather fight it out." I say, looking straight ahead.

"Well, that wasn't too bright of them," says Jane with a smile. She says she doesn't approve of fighting, but she's too proud of my ability to win fights to really be upset with me.

Chapter 3

Cody and Jesse walk their hoses over to the corral and size up the horses there. I told them to pick out some pack horses to help take the fencing material up to the hidden valley. They picked out two horses and started loading them up with the material, as I watched them, I heard someone calling me from over by the path. I turned to see Kent, one of my newer hands riding over to me.

"Boss" said Kent, "there's some people coming up the trail." I get up on my horse and ride over to the trail. There are five men coming up the trail. I guess that the head of the lazy K has decided to take me up on my invitation. As I ride over toward them, my boys and a few of the hands come over to give me some support.

"Good morning" I say, as friendly as could be, "welcome to the Rocking A. My name is…"

"I don't much care" says a man in the group, interrupting me. I assume by his stature that he's the one in charge. "I hear that you beat up one of my men."

"Who are you?" I ask.

"Name's Thompson" says the man, "I own the Lazy K ranch."

"I hear that makes us neighbors." I say with a smile. This doesn't seem to impress Thompson much.

"Neighbors don't go beating up their neighbors' hands," Thompson says with a scowl. Now I would normally have just agreed to this type of sentiment, but since circumstances were what they were, I'm not going to give him the satisfaction.

"Now, circumstances being…" I start before he steps in again. Manners obviously aren't his strong point.

"I don't care much about circumstances; you beat my man." His horse steps closer to me and I notice that Lassiter is at the back of the group. His jaw is bruised up, but he doesn't look beat. I've looked like that after winning some fights.

"Well," I say looking at Lassiter, "your man has a fast mouth and slow whit. I didn't so much as beat him as outsmarted him." Thompson chuckles a little at this, which irks Lassiter. Thompson looks back at Lassiter then returns his gaze to me.

"I see," he finally says, "I suppose he isn't as smart as some, but he's a good hand."

"I'm sure he is," I agree "but I still don't take to having men calling me old." Thompson looks back at Lassiter again, I suppose Lassiter wouldn't tell his boss the whole story. I sense a shift in Thompson's attitude, so I decide now was a good time to try some civility, "now, I've been wanting to talk to you, as we are neighbors. You're welcome up to my place for some coffee." He doesn't seem too sure, so I decide to add some encouragement, "My wife, made flapjacks, I imagine there's some left."

This seems to have the desired effect, he smiles and tells me to lead the way. As we ride to the house, I tell Cody to take Thomson's men to the bunkhouse and offer some hospitality. We dismount in front of the house and hand our horses over to the hands. Thompson looks up at the house with some appreciation. We walk into the sitting room, and I offer the well-dressed man a seat. He stands a few inches shorter than me, as he removes his hat, I can see that his hair is dark and about shoulder length. His dark beard is neatly trimmed though. I walk through to the kitchen.

"Jane" I call out as I enter the dining area, on the way to the kitchen, "we have company." I don't make it to the kitchen before Jane comes out with a coffee pot in her hand. Emily following close behind with a tray holding some of Jane's best china, and a plate with piping hot flapjacks. Obviously, someone has warned her we might have company, she never ceases to amaze me.

"Hello," says Jane "I'm Jane Locke, Henry's wife and this is our daughter Emily. Won't you please come to the table for some food and coffee?" As she says this, Emily is setting two places at the table. Our stunned guest walks over to the table, looking at the hot flapjacks a little hungrily.

"Morning Ma'am" he says as he sits. "Thank you for this, I did not realize how hungry I was until just now." I sit down as Emily serves out the food and hot coffee. The two ladies then slip out all smiles and feminine charm, I felt a very lucky man. While I had already eaten I rarely say no to a second breakfast, so I tuck into my food. Thompson does the same, we eat for a minute in silence, sizing each other up as we enjoy our food.

"So," I open the conversation, "what brings you to Colorado?"
"Land, mostly" says Thompson, slowing down his eating and turning to his coffee. "It's going cheap." He gives me a small grin and sits back to enjoy his drink. He's not wrong, what with the gold veins drying up, people were selling their claims for cheap.

"I've heard you bought a large plot of land," I'm leading him to find out if people are telling the truth about what he is saying in town.

"Yeah, but it's mostly slopes, not a lot of good grazing land," he tells me. "But I think I can manage a few hundred head. Not a large herd, but enough for me to be comfortable, I think."

"I've heard you come right up to my property line," I'm still probing.

"I believe that's right, my property comes up to Morrison's Pass, I've heard that's your line." So, the rumors were true, but the way he just out and says it to me leads me to believe that he isn't aware that I own a quarter of that land. I take a deep breath to steady myself.

"Who sold you all that land?" I ask slowly.

"What do you mean by that?" he says indignantly. I guess I took a bad approach to this conversation.

"I'm just asking, because I reckon someone cheated you, I own everything from Shy's Creek to Morrison's Pass." I'm trying to keep everything calm but I can see it isn't working as he is starting to turn red.

"I was told everything was empty to Morrison's pass," he's put the cup down and is leaning forward.

"It was," I'm trying to let him know I don't blame him for any misunderstanding.

"However, I just bought that land, and all the paperwork is filed with the land office."

"Maybe someone cheated you," he's starting to rise out of his chair, "did you think of that?"

"I knew the previous owner of that land well and we did everything by the law." He is on his feet now, so I slowly rise to meet him face to face. We are looking across the table at each other, I'm trying to keep my temper in check, but he obviously doesn't feel the need to do that.

"Well, that land is mine now," he says slowly, "if I see anyone from your outfit on my land…" he glowers at me, expecting me to back down.

"There is no call for threats or violence," I say, holding up my hands at chest level. "I'm sure we can work this all out. I have a copy of the deed here if you'd like to look at it."

"The lands mine and that it," he says as he turns abruptly to leave. "You just keep off it!" I try to continue to talk, but he rushes out the door, calling loudly for his men. I watch, feeling a bit helpless as they mount up and ride off down the path.

Cody walks over to me, looking at the men ride off. "Looks like that didn't go well," he says.

"Nope," I say, "we best keep out of the hidden valley until I've had a chance to square things away with the authorities. The law is on our side." Jane comes out the front door and gives me a knowing look.

"I heard everything," she says, "you did the best you could, what's the next step?"

"I'm going to head to the Sherrif," I say slowly, "show him my copy of the deed." It's the sheriff's job to settle matters like this, so I'll give him a chance.

I walk over to the house and Jane and Cody follow me inside. Emily is already clearing off the table, a serious look on her face. Cody goes to a cabinet to get a cup for some of the leftover coffee. He pours himself a cup and sits at the table.

I walk over to a small room I added off the living room a few years back. It was Cody's idea to have a space dedicated to all the paperwork required to run the place, called it the Ranch Office, which sounded a bit too high-faultin for the likes of me, but I came to like having a private place to sit and think. The deed for the new land was still on the desk in there, I hadn't gotten around to finding it a place.

I bring the deed out and place it on the table. Cody picks it up and looks it over as I get my hat and coat on. He hands it to me without saying anything and follows me out as I walk back out to the barn for my horse.

"Cody" I say to him as he catches up to me, "tell everyone to put up the fencing and then get to their daily tasks." Cody nods and walks over to the bunkhouse. There is a group of hands standing in the doorway trying to figure out what is going on. There aren't many secrets on a small ranch.

Chapter 4

It's still morning as I ride into Victor, and the town is quiet. There aren't many people bustling around, but there are a few horses at the saloon. I ride over to the Sheriff's office and tie up Little Red out front before going into the office. It's a small building, a small office with a desk, stove in the corner and two holding cells in the back. There's someone in one of the cells, probably sleeping off a good time at the saloon. Sheriff Kenedy doesn't tolerate drunken fools starting any trouble. He's saved a few lives by putting them in a cell before their big mouth got them shot.

Kenedy stands up at his desk as I walk in, "Locke" he says as I come in, "what's up?" I'm not a regular at the Sheriff's office anymore, so he's curious why I'm here. He indicates a chair across from him at the desk and we sit.

"I just met with Thompson," I say as soon as I'm seated, "owner of the Lazy K."

"I see," Kenedy says leaning back in his chair "how did that go?"

"You were right," I tell him, "he's under the impression that he owns everything up to Morrison's Pass." Kenedy picks up a tobacco pouch from his desk and starts to roll himself a cigarette. "I thought it best to show you my copy off the deed since he doesn't seem to believe me." I hand him the deed, and he takes a good look at it before placing it on his desk.

"What do you expect might happen?" he asks me.

"I'm not sure," I say "but he made some threats. He isn't much interested in my legal claim."

"I see" says Kenedy, "well I suppose I can keep my ears open. It looks legal, but then things can be forged."

"You calling that a forgery?" I ask, leaning toward him.

"Not exactly," Kenedy says, holding up one hand, "I'm just being cautious. Land claims can be tricky."

"I know," I rebut, pointing to the deed "that's why the land office hands these out." Kenedy considers that for a minute as he smokes his cigarette. He stands up and walks over to the cell and looks in at the man sleeping in there. He turns back with a worried look on his face.

"Look," he says "I've known you for a long time. You're a good man, and I know that." He pauses for a moment and then sits back down at his desk. "I don't want a land war here, and it looks like everything is official, but I want to be careful. I'm going to write to the land office for confirmation. Until then, can you wait to move onto that land?"

"I suppose," I say thoughtfully, "but I'm not sure Thompson will promise the same."

"I'll talk to him," Kenedy says confidently, "he'll listen to reason." I'm not too sure about that, Thompson doesn't seem a reasonable man, but I also respect the law and decide to give Kenedy the chance to do things his way.

"You talk to him." I say, "I'll wait on word from you before I start to move cattle." Kenedy thanks me, he knows this is a hard thing to ask of me. I stand up and head out to my horse.

As I mount Little Red, I notice the sun is almost overhead. Half a day wasted on this nonsense; I was hoping to have a good start on my fencing by now. I'm a patient man, but I've been known to be frustrated when behind schedule, I only have so long to get things done before winter hits and winters here are long and harsh.

As I ride out of town, I get this sense that I'm being watched. I look around and see a man by the saloon, leaning against the wall, but he is looking away from me. There is nobody else around, so I guess I'm just being nervous. It's noon, I've had a long day and nothing has been accomplished, that's throwing off my senses.

As I come around a bend in the trail there are three men on horseback, guns drawn. I recognize one as Lassiter, but don't know the other two. I take a quick second to decide between talk and action but decide that Lassiter isn't likely to be here to talk things through. To prove me right, Lassiter fires at me and I feel the bullet graze my left cheek.

I turn Red to the right as I slide off her right flank. I palm my revolver on the way to the ground. I slap her flank as I jump into the tree line, creating some confusion as she runs the opposite direction of my jump. As I hit the tree line, I hear more shots and Red whinny as she is hit. I turn to face the riders and take quick aim. I'm not much for gunfights anymore, but I've always been very accurate with my shots. Growing up my Pa told me to make sure every shot counted when hunting, he taught me bringing a deer down with one shot was better than spending a day trailing a wounded deer.

My first shot hits one of the men dead center of his chest and he falls off his horse without making a sound. He's dead before hitting the ground. The two other men look around to where my shot came from, confused because they hadn't seen me jump behind this tree. I am already on the move though, crouching behind some tall grass until I find a fallen tree to hide behind.

"Lassiter!" I shout, "stop being a fool, put your gun up and head out." Lassiter's head snaps around to look for where my voice is coming from. I'm on the move again back to where I started. Lassiter slides off his horse and rushes towards where I was. He shoots at the felled tree, and I can hear the slugs hit the wood. Since the other man kept to his horse, I take aim and shot the man in the shoulder.

He grunts and falls sideways, catching himself before he hits the ground.

As I move again, I can see Red limping down the trail, so obviously she's been shot in the leg. I'll have to walk her home, but hopefully she'll be ok. I can't see Lassiter anymore, but his partner is calling out to him.

"Lassiter!" his partner says "I'm hit, Jones is dead. Let's just get out of here." I can see the leaves move where I was when fired the last shot. He's looking for me.

"He's right Lassiter," I yell out, "you can't win." I move again, quietly moving through the long grass. I'm not really being as quiet as I should, but Lassiter seems to have very little skill in tracking people. I suppose he's used to having a standoff in town and not in the wild. "Tell you what," from my new vantage point. I can see Lassiter now moving through the grass, "I'll let you load up your friend and get out of here."

"Go to the devil" says Lassiter, I see his gun come up as he shoots in my general direction, but he again he doesn't find his target. I return fire, without as careful an aim and hear Lassiter grunt as I do find my target. I see him fall.

"Lassiter?" cries out the last man standing, "you, alright?"

"No! I'm not alright," I guess I didn't manage to kill him, he then cussed me out before asking his friend to help him out of there. His partner waited another second, obviously trying to take stock of the situation.

"Hey Locke," he yelled in my general direction, "you ok if I get him?" It was nice to be in charge of the situation. I yell out my assent and watch the man get off his horse and walk through the grass. He helps Lassiter stand up and helps him walk through the trees to the trail. I can see that I had hit Lassiter in the gut, and he is bleeding badly.

The man tries hard to help Lassiter on his horse, but he keeps falling over. It's not easy to help someone onto a horse when he's gut shot and you're nursing a shoulder. I put my gun away and walk out of the trees towards the men. Lassiter glares at me and reaches for his gun but his partner stops him.

"You want to live?" the man says quietly and then turned to me and said, "I know I don't have any right to ask, but can you help?" I suppose old age has softened me up some, I go over and help Lassiter on the horse, him glowering at me the whole time.

"Let's get your buddy out of the dirt too," I say. We walk over to the dead man and the two of us manage to drape him over his horse. The wounded man then thanks me, takes the reins of the dead man's horse before mounting his own horse and starting off down the trail.

"This isn't he last of this," Lassiter says as his horse starts to follow.

"If you're smart it will be," I threaten as they ride off. I go over to Red as they are riding and get my canteen, while watching the men disappear, I take a drink from my canteen. After they are out of sight, I use the canteen water to wash off Red's wound. It wasn't bleeding too much, so I packed some grass over it and took the reins in my hand and started the long walk home. I might be home before sunset, but this day was wasted now.

Chapter 5

It seems I now get into more trouble from my daughter for letting her favorite horse get shot, than from my wife for getting into a gun fight. To be fair I didn't really ask for either. It's early morning and Emily is already out in the barn tending to Little Red's wound. Jane spent a few minutes tutting over last night, caring for the graze wound on my face. It wasn't deep enough to leave a scar, which made her happy enough.

As I'm eating breakfast with Jane, Cody comes to the table and sits across from me. He was ready to mount up a bunch of hands to take off after the Lazy K men last night. I'm still not sure Lassiter wasn't lashing out on his own after his embarrassment yesterday morning. Of course, this morning I'm a little concerned about Thompson. He came looking for blood when I punched one of his hands, I can't imagine how he will respond to me shooting three of them.

"Pa?" Cody starts, "I think it would be best if you let me or Jesse ride with you today." Cody is thinking the same thing as I am.

"I'll manage," I say with a smile, "I took care of myself pretty well yesterday."

"Don't get cocky," says my supportive wife, "you're too old to be getting into gun fights." She is right about that; I decided twenty years ago to stop getting into fights.

"This wasn't my fault," I say with a smile, "they ambushed me." Jane gives me a look and then shakes her head and sighs. "Tell you what," I continue, "let's spend the morning checking the fence along Morrison's Pass." Jane is giving me one of her looks again. "We can't have any cattle getting onto the disputed land," I add looking at Jane with a sly grin, "I promised Kenedy I would wait until he has a chance to verify my deed." This is the first Cody has heard of this, I gave Jane the full rundown of the day last night when we were in bed. He looks at me indignantly and stands up.

"You said what?" he says, "Pa, that land is ours, free and clear."

"You speak to your father with some respect," Jane says sternly.

"Sorry Ma," he says sheepishly, "sorry Pa."

I stand up to look my son in the eyes, "the land office will support my claim. Can't blame a lawman for making sure he's upholding the law properly." I give my wife a kiss goodbye and lead my son out the door to get to work.

When I get to the barn, Emily is there with Little Red. She has bandaged up her wound as best as she could. Last night a couple of the hands helped hold her down so we could put some salve on her. She is limping around a bit this morning but doesn't seem too bothered. Emily, however, is still grumbling about those fools who shot her baby. I saddle up Boots, who is a fair substitute for Red.

We gather a group of men who don't have any other responsibilities and go out to check the fence line. As we ride the fence along the pass, we can see that there are very few places that need mending. Here and there a fallen branch or tree has knocked some wire loose, but it all of these are a quick fix.

A few hours later we start to head back toward the house. Boot's ears suddenly perk up in the direction we are headed. As I look up ahead, I can see a few men on the other side of the fence just watching us. As I ride closer, I can see Thompson sitting on his horse amongst the men. I ride up to them and stop when I get to them. I motion to my men to stand back. I know Cody will be watching for trouble and trust my men to back me up if trouble starts.

"Morning" I say to Thompson. Thomson looks at me angrily and turns to the fellow I had helped load up a dead body about 24 hours ago. His arm was in a sling, and he was looking a bit green. I suppose Thompson likes to bring my victims along to show me my sins. I turn to the man in the sling, "how's Lassiter?" I ask.

"He'll live," says the man. Thompson shakes his head at the man as if to tell him to be seen and not heard.

"You killed one of my men," Thompson says in a low, threatening voice.

"They shot first," I answer quickly, "and it was three against one. I wasn't looking for trouble with Lassiter, but I suppose he got some friends together to find trouble with me." Thompson's expression let me know my assumption was wrong.

"I warned you yesterday to stay on your land," he says quickly.

"I am on my land," I say and then quickly add "you're on my land too." This is probably a good way to start a fight, but to my reasoning, the fight was coming either way. I can sense Cody riding up closer to me. A glance tells me he has his rifle across his saddle. "I know you haven't had a chance to talk to the Sheriff, but he's not wanting us to fight and is contacting the land office..." I don't get to finish this sentence as Thompson starts getting riled up.

"Land office?" he practically shouts, "what the hell for?"

Calmly I look at him and then say, "to check my deed against yours, I imagine he'll be wanting to see yours." Again, this news wasn't hitting Thompson right, he turns his horse around.

"We'll have to see about that," he says as he rides up the pass. The rest of the men from the Lazy K slowly turn and follow him. Cody quietly puts its rifle back into the sheath on his saddle.

"I bet he has no deed," says Cody.

"If not, the Sheriff will find that out quickly and should solve all our problems," I say with a smile. Cody doesn't look so sure.

"Pa," he says as we turn to ride home, "this guy Thompson is bad news."

"Yeah," I say thoughtfully "he is."

"I doubt he's going to go down without a fight."

"Then it will be a fight," I stop my horse and Cody does the same, "if the Sheriff can't convince him to back off, we will be ready." I then turned to the hands riding with us, there were five men which is about half of all the men we had working for us. "Boys, I've worked a ranch in a land war before. It's not a good thing for anyone. If this comes to a fight, and any of you want out, you let me know. Pass word among the others too. I know you are all good men, and true, but this isn't your fight. You want to leave; I'll pay out your wages and there will be no hard feelings." The men look at me thoughtfully and we turn back toward the house.

As we ride up to the house, I can see Jane on front porch watching. That woman knows how to worry. I ride up to the house and Jane stands up, her hands knitted together in front of her. She smiles but her worries are obvious.

I get off my horse and hand the reins to Cody. I walk over to Jane and give her a hug before leading her into the house. I know she needs to know everything that happens, but it is probably better to tell her in the comfort of her own sitting room. After I tell her the whole story she sits quietly, obviously thinking things over.

"I don't think he has any papers for the property," she says.

"That's likely the truth," I say "but it's best to let Kenedy investigate it. I am not a popular man over at the Lazy K." I smile at Jane and she gives me one of her looks.

"Can we trust Kenedy?" she asks.

"I think so," I say, "he's always done right by me." Jane looks at me and then looks towards the open door as Cody comes into the house.

"Pa," says Cody, coming in and sitting on a wooden chair by the hearth, which is sitting unused on this warm day, "I passed on your message to the other men."

"What message?" Jane asks.

"I told the men if this comes to a land war," I say, "and I'm not saying it will, but if it does, I will not resent any man that wants to be paid off and head out."

"I suppose that's only right," says Jane.

"The men all want you to know they appreciate what you said," Cody continues, "but they are Rocking A men and will stand for her if need be." This surprises me a little, I know most of the men are true to the brand, but we have some men who haven't been here long. Loyalty builds over time, I don't expect it in any man I haven't known long.

"Tell the men I am thankful," I say, I pause for a moment to find the right words, "I will do what I can to prevent a fight, but life has taught me that sometimes the fight comes no matter what."

Chapter 6

It is getting warmer; the summer weather is finally getting up to where we are. I'm riding out to the field where most of our herd is grazing to check on everything. After a stressful few days, it feels good to be getting back into my normal routine. We have several hundred head out here, and I can tell by the looks of them that we will be seeing some calves soon. Jesse is riding out amongst the herd, so I ride over to talk to him.

As we are discussing the plans for calving season, I'm enjoying the smell of the cows. It's an earthy smell that feels comfortable to me; I've been a cattle man for a long time now and something about it calms me. I can feel the tension shift off my shoulders as we get a plan together for the next few weeks. I know we will need to get to the hidden valley to fence it in before winter, but right now I feel confident that it will all work out somehow.

Off in the distance I see a rider coming from the direction of Morrison's Pass. He's coming down a steep slope into the valley we are in, and the way his horse is gingerly stepping, I know it can't be one of my horses, my horses know that slope well and move down it with confidence. As the rider gets closer, I can see that it is the Sheriff, and I can feel myself getting more tense. Not wanting to prolong the inevitable. Jessie is riding beside me, ready for trouble.

As I get closer, I see the worried face of Sheriff Kenedy. I raise a hand in greeting, he waves back as his horse hits more level ground. I can start to feel the tension start to rise.

"Henry," he says as we are close enough to talk, "I'm glad I found you." He rides a bit closer and we stop, our horses making a semi-circle so we can talk.

"Good to see you Sheriff," I say, "what brings you out here."

"I just met with Thompson over at the Lazy K" he says, "I wanted to see if I could help you work out a peaceful solution." It's nice to know he's a man of his word.

"How'd that go?" I think I know the answer, but deep down I have a small hope that Kenedy could reason with the man.

"Not well," Kenedy says, "that man seems to have a chip on his shoulder. All I did was ask him to take some time before using the land you have a claim to." The Sheriff stops to pull out his canteen and take a drink, it's been a long day and I'm sure he's hoping for something a bit stronger than water. "I asked him if I could see his copy of the deed and he told me to go to hell. I don't think he has one and is hoping to bully his way onto the land." He pauses for a moment, looking around at all the cattle before continuing, "he told me you ambushed some of his men the other day, killed one and shot two more."

"They ambushed me," I tell him, "I was riding back from town. They were waiting around the bend a mile from town."

"Three men ambushed you, and you get away unharmed?" he asks with some obvious suspicion.

"They can't aim," I say slowly. "You can still see where they grazed me," I point to my cheek, "and they hit my horse."

"I know your reputation," says the Sheriff, "I loved hearing stories of the Appalachian Kid growing up, but ambushed by three younger men and walking away? That's a lot to believe."

"Those stories were mostly made up," I tell him. I had developed a reputation for gun fighting as a young man after coming down from the hills. I had left the hills after a long family feud ended up destroying two families, mine included. I was young and angry with the world, so I took it out on anyone that crossed me.

"I just don't want any more violence," Kenedy says looking at me, "If you have a legal claim to that land, then you have a right to take it." I nod at the sheriff, and he looks around for another minute gathering his thoughts. "Look," he continues, "I can't really tell you what to do here. I wrote to the land office and I should hear back in a couple of weeks. I'd appreciate it if you stayed away from him and kept the peace. I'll take your word about the ambush for now, because I know you and can't believe that even with your reputation that you would do something like that." He is looking at the ground in thought, trying to make sense of everything as he speaks.

"I'd like to start getting that land ready for winter," I start and Kenedy looks up at me.

"It appears they are already doing that," Kenedy blurts out, "when I found them, they had found a nice, secluded spot on the disputed land, looks like they are putting up some corrals and a small cabin."

"I see," I say, I'm not sure what to think about this. I have a purpose for that land, but a small cabin wouldn't be a huge problem, in fact it might be nice if the winter gets too cold, someone could stay up there and watch things. "I'd hate to take anything from the man, but if he wants to build on my land, that's his mistake."

"Only a fool builds on land he doesn't own," adds Jesse.

"While that's true," I say, "a lot of people have staked claims by building. I'm sure he's hoping someone will just let him have the land since he's living on it."

"The land needs to be free of claims for that to work," says Jesse.

"Very true son," says Kenedy, "that's the law and I will uphold it." The sheriff looks at the cattle again and sighs. He finally looks back at me, "you're a good man Locke, I'll do what I can to back you up if it comes to trouble."

“You’re a good man too,” I say with all sincerity, “I don’t want any more trouble than I’ve already had. I gave all that up a long time ago and enjoy the peaceful life.

Chapter 7

The sun is getting low as I ride back to the house. Jesse had gone on ahead a while ago, and I was enjoying the quiet of the evening. All that talk of my reputation brought back a lot of memories. When I was young and angry I joined in any fight that would have me. My reputation grew because I was good at what I did. I enjoyed having a reputation as well, but as I aged, I learned that hard work was more rewarding than picking fights.

Then I met Jane while working on a ranch down on the high planes. While she was a beauty beyond compare, she also had common sense. She talked about settling down and having a family and it all made sense the way she put it. Then when Cody was born, I never looked back, being someone's father just made me feel better than I ever did as a fighter.

I reach the house and ride over to the barn. I get off the paint and lead him into his stall. I take his saddle off and start giving him a good run-down. After I finish that I get him some grain and put it into his trough. He's had a hard ride today and seems happy to be home. As I start to walk out, I see Emily in with Little Red, so I walk over to them.

"How's she doing?" I ask. Emily turns to me and smiles, she's forgiven me for getting her baby shot, but barely.

"She's taking more food today," Emily says. I must still be feeling a bit nostalgic as I look at Emily, because I know she's getting close to womanhood, but I still expect her to crawl up into my lap when scared. Here she is taking some responsibility and nursing my horse back to health.

I smile at her and say, "well I'd say she's got the best nurse she could have." I give Emily a hug and kiss the top of her head. Even in this environment I can smell her perfume, the same lavender water her mother uses. I'm going to have a job keeping men away from her.

Cody walks into the barn and over to us. "Pa" he says, "there's some kid up at the house. Says he needs to talk with you."

"Kid?" I ask.

"Yes, about thirteen or fourteen I'd guess." Cody says, "he's ridden a long way by the looks of him. He asked for you by name." Cody isn't too much older at twenty, so I chuckle at him calling someone a kid. Emily trails behind us a little as we go to the house.

As we enter the house, I see a thin boy sitting at the table, Jane has already brought him some food. The kid has long, straggly blonde hair, a worn sunburned face and is wearing a leather coat that is much older than he is. He stands up respectfully as I enter the house and I see his eye wander over to Emily.

"Hello lad," I say as I enter, "Cody says you want to see me?" I indicate that he should sit again and I sit in my spot at the head of the table. "Emily," I say over my shoulder, "would you mind getting me a plate as well?" Emily nods and walks over to the kitchen, she seems to be watching the boy with one eye as she walks by.

"Yes sir," says the boy, "my name is Silas Trent, I've been told you might be the person to help me out." Emily arrives with my food and puts it in front of me. She then walks over to a broom sitting in the corner and starts sweeping a floor that I know full well has been swept at least twice today.

"That depends on what you need," I say cautiously. I take a bite of my food and look at this kid, Silas. He is covered in dust from the trail; it looks like he's been out there for weeks.

"I'm looking to kill Jack Thompson," says the boy, squaring his jaw. I'm a little taken aback, but I just take another bite, waiting for him to continue. "The shopkeeper in Victor said you've already killed two of his men. I figure you're the man to come see about finding him and finishing him off."

Jane has poured me a beer and offers it to me. I take a long drink and then look at Silas. "Son," I say, "you've got the wrong man. Why do you want Thompson dead?"

"He killed my family," says the boy bluntly.

"I see," I take another drink, "and how did he do that?"

"He was rustling our cattle," Silas says, "he was caught red handed. When we were chasing him down, he got the drop on my Pa and brother and killed them both."

"How do you know it was him?" Cody asks from the entryway to the dining where he's leaning against a post and listening to everything.

"He shot me and left me for dead." Silas lifts his shirt and exposes a ragged red scar right below his lower rib on his right side. I hear a slight gasp from Emily, I look up and she has her hand covering her gaping mouth. Silas sees her too, "sorry ma'am." he says looking over to Jane, tucking his shirt back in as best he can while sitting. "I forgot there were ladies present." Obviously, someone taught him some manners.

"Where's your Ma?" Jane says sitting next to Silas, her mother's instinct has kicked in. It won't be easy if I want to rid myself of this lad now. Emily has put the broom down and sits as well, all pretense of cleaning is gone.

"She's at home," Silas says to her, "she's ok. She told me not to come after Thompson when I was up and moving again, but I snuck off."

"She's right," I tell the boy, "seeking revenge is a loser's game." Silas' shoulders slump and he looks down at his now empty plate. "My advice is to head home and help your Ma run your place."

"That's just it," says the boy, "we have nothing left to run. After killing my Pa, Thompson took all our cattle and hightailed it out of there." I sit back in my seat and look at the boy.

"What's your brand son?" I ask quietly.

"The Lazy K," he replies. "We have a ranch down by Goldfield in Arizona." Thompson didn't even change the brand, just moved that cattle to where no one had heard of them. It is becoming more obvious to me that Thompson is going to remain a thorn in my side.

"Cody," I say, turning to my son, "what do you think?" Cody sits at the table and grabs a slice of bread from the loaf situated in the middle of the table. He slathers it with butter before looking at me.

"Well, if this lad is telling the truth," he puts a hand up before Silas can object, "and I believe he is, I think we need to talk to the Sheriff."

"We'd need some proof," I say thoughtfully, "Silas, did your Pa have a brand certificate?"

"Yes" says the boy, "I have a certified copy in my saddle bag."

"Then we have the proof we need," I say with a smile, "if you would like to spend the night in the bunkhouse, we can head into town in the morning." I stand up to take the boy out.

"Thank you, sir," says Silas, standing as well "it's been a few weeks since I left home."

"How old are you, Silas?" asks Jane. I look over at her and frown.

"I'm fourteen," he says.

"Pretty young to be out for revenge," says.

"I can take care of myself, missus," says Silas as he starts to follow me out, "thank you for the food, it was the best I've had in a while." Silas and I walked out into the yard, and I lead him over to the bunkhouse.

When we get inside the bunkhouse, I show him an empty bunk and where he can find a pump for water and the outhouse. He stands there by the bunk for a minute and looks at me.

“Mister?” he finally says, “do you really think the law can help?” He looked sure of himself in the house, but now he looks like a scared child.

“Silas,” I say, putting a hand on his shoulder, it’s now that I realize he is short for his age, barely four and a half feet, “the sheriff here is a good man. If he can help, he will.” Silas looks down at the floor, he looks like he is about to cry then straightens his back and looks back at me.

“Thank you sir,” he says, “I think my Pa would like you.”

“Well, he’s raised a good man in you,” I say, “I’m sure I would have liked him too. I’ll let you get washed up and rest, we will get an early start in the morning.” Silas sighs and sinks down onto his bunk. I walk out quickly to give him a moment to grieve.

Chapter 8

The next morning as I walk into the dining area, a freshly cleaned Silas is sitting at the table. He stands up as soon as he sees me.

"Good morning, sir," he says as I walk in, "Emily invited me in for breakfast." Of course she did, Emily takes after her mother a little too much. "I got this for you to see." He holds up a document packet and pushes it across the table to my spot.

I sit down and open it up. It is all the registration paperwork for the Lazy K brand, registered to Cole Trent, who must be Silas' father. Everything looked legal, Thompson must have stolen the cattle from Trent and brought it up here, figuring nobody would follow. I must hand it to the boy, he has done well to think about bringing the papers to support his claims. I'm not sure I would have thought of doing that at his age.

The kitchen door opens and Emily comes through the door with a big smile. "I hope you like bacon and eggs," she says cheerfully and then stops when she sees me sitting in my spot. She smiles sheepishly and places a plate with some bacon and fried eggs. “I have your plate about ready too, Pa” she adds before rushing back into the kitchen. If I’m not mistaken, she is wearing the ready-made dress they bought last week.

Silas sits patiently waiting for Emily to bring me some food. I tell him to get started, certain that Emily’s not being fully truthful about my food being nearly ready. He wolfs down his food, I can’t help but wonder what he’s been eating on the trail. He has a short barreled colt on his hip, so he had the ability to catch some game. He’s awfully skinny though, so he might not have had much luck. I’ve known some lean times on the trail when food is hard to come by.

Cody and Jesse come out of their room and Jesse sits at the table as Cody walks into the kitchen. A minute later Emily comes out with my plate and some coffee. She looks at Jesse and asks him if he wants anything, he tells her what he wants and she heads back. She is wearing her nicer dress today. I shake my head, I’m not ready for her to start trying to get the attention of boys.

I notice that Silas has a sad smile on his face, it must be hard to be back in family life after such a tragedy broke up his own. Cody comes out with his own plate and some coffee. He sits next to Silas and starts eating.

"Silas," Cody says, "I was looking at your pony, he looks good."

"Thanks," Silas says "he's a good horse, but not too surefooted in these hills. I almost took a spill a couple of days back that could have be bad."

"Desert horses don't do too well up here," I say, "it's a rocky trail into town, we can let you ride one of our mountain horses." As I finished saying this Jane came through the door from the kitchen, she had been listening, I'm sure.

"I was thinking we could all go into town," she says, "give Silas some moral support." A mama bear has nothing on Jane, so I agree that's a good idea, it would be foolish not to. "I'll pack a picnic lunch, and we can stop off at the creek on the way back." She has been thinking about this for a while, likely already has the picnic ready to go.

"Sounds good," I say, amused, "I'll go hitch up the wagon when I'm done eating." Jane walks over and puts her hand on my shoulder, giving me a loving look. I know what she's thinking, she'll give Silas some sense of normality while he's here.

I hand the packet of paperwork over to Silas and stand up to go get things ready for the trip. I head out to the barn and start getting the wagon ready. After a minute Cody and Jesse come out to start saddling the horses, they aren't fans of the wagon, and I don't blame them, the rocky trail makes the ride very uncomfortable. I tell them to saddle Boots for Silas.

As I'm finishing up Emily walks out with Silas close behind, he is carrying the basket for the picnic. She walks over to the wagon and directs Silas in placing it in a secure place in the back. Silas offers her a hand and helps her up into the wagon. She is beaming. Jane is the last out, making sure she closes the door to the house tight before walking over.

Cody leads the paint over to Silas who mounts him easily. He's very comfortable with horses. It's been a while since the whole family has gone to town together, I'm feeling very proud of my little group.

A few hours later our group arrives in town. The town is busy today, I can see a couple of wagons in front of the general store being loaded and several people milling around.

Adam spots me from the front stoop of his store and waves. He spots Silas riding with us and rushes over to flag us down.

"I see he found you," Adam says, looking up at me in my seat in the wagon.

"Yes," I affirm "we're bringing him to meet Sheriff Kenedy."

"Oh, I see," he says a bit concerned. I'm not going to add to the rumor mill right now, so I urge the horses forward toward the sheriff's office. I wave to Adam as we head on, wishing him a good day.

Sheriff Kenedy is in his office as we ride in. Jane and I escort Silas into the office while our children loiter outside. The office is empty except for Kenedy who is sitting at his desk, feet up, hat over his eyes, taking a quick nap. As we come in, he jumps up, startled awake by our footsteps.

"Locke!" he exclaims, "what's going on?" He looks at the rest of my group and removes his hat. "Mrs. Locke, it's always a pleasure to have you here." He rushes around the desk to dust off a chair and offers it to her.

He invites Silas and I to sit after dragging a third chair in front of his desk. After we are settled, I start the introductions.

"Kenedy, this young man is Silas Trent," I start, "he has some information about the Lazy K outfit I think you need to see."

"Ok," says Kenedy, "how do you know this young man?"

"He heard I took on and killed two men from Thompson's outfit and figured me for an ally," I say.

"Only one man as far as I've heard," says Kenedy, "Lassiter is still alive."

Silas' head whipped over to look at me, "you shot Tom Lassiter?" he asks in shock.

"I suppose so," I say, unsure why this got a rise from the boy.

"He's a legend in our parts," says the boy, "they say he's killed at least five men in fair fights. My brother saw him take down two men in a single fight once. Said his draw was a blur."

"I've never seen his quick draw, what I have seen is his poor aim. Anyway," I add to change the subject, "this lad says he's the rightful owner of the Lazy K brand, and all the cattle belong to his outfit."

Kenedy looks over at the kid and smiles, "he owns the brand?" he asks.

"By right of inheritance," I say, "seems Thompson and his men killed his father and older brother before taking all their cattle."

"I see," Kenedy looks over at Silas, "do you have any evidence?"

"Just what I saw," says Silas.

"You were there?" asks the sheriff.

"He has the scars to prove it" Jane interjects, "they left him for dead and rode off." Kenedy looks over at Jane, he doesn't know her too well and has never seen her upset before.

"That's interesting," he says, "what about the stolen cattle?"

"He has a brand registration certificate," I tell him. "It's from Arizona but shows that his Pa owns the Lazy K brand." I show him the certificate, and he looks at it intently.

"Well son," he says looking at the certificate, "I've seen those cattle and the brand matches what you have here. So, your Pa owns the cattle. Of course, if he is dead..."

"Which he is" I interject.

"Yes," continues the sheriff, he then has a realization "don't you have a mother?"

"Yes, sir I do," Silas says quietly.

"Then she inherits some of the cattle," Kenedy says thoughtfully, "but I guess that doesn't change the fact that they are stolen." Kenedy starts his routine in rolling a cigarette, he is in deep thought. "Ok," he finally says, "I need to go up there and arrest Thompson, I'll grab some deputies. Since you have a history with the man, I need you to keep away until the judge gets here." He looks at a calendar on his wall, "which is in a couple of weeks."

I agree with the sheriff and thank him for acting on this. We will have to deal with caring for the cattle and returning it after the court case, but that's a problem for another day. Silas looks from the sheriff to me; he obviously has a question.

"What happens when the judge gets here?" Silas asks.

"There is a trial and you will have to give testimony against him," says the sheriff, "he will probably be found guilty. If so, he will be hung."

"So long as he dies," Silas says quietly. He's hell bent on revenge and I can't say that I blame him. I know the feeling of seeing your father shot down, I was there when the feud took my Pa from me. I went on the warpath too, but all it brought me was years of misery. I'm hoping to save Silas from the same.

As we head out to the wagon, I can see Adam standing by our wagon, talking to Cody. I'm sure he is pressing him for details, so he has all the gossip. As I reach the wagon, Adam smiles at me.

"So, it is true that some of Thompson's men jumped you," he says victoriously, "I knew that story about you ambushing them couldn't be true." Adam will now tell the whole town my side of the story, which will only increase the legend of local gunfighter, the Appalachian Kid took on three young gunslingers and won, and him almost fifty years old.

Chapter 9

Silas Trent is a hard worker. He's been here a week now and has found a place among the hands and is part of the daily routine of the ranch. Every day he asks quietly if there's been news from the sheriff, and I'm starting to wonder myself what is going on. Kenedy has always been a careful man, he'll get a group of deputies together before heading out. I figured it would be a day or two, but not a week.

I'm standing on my front porch, looking at the men coming back from the fields. I wish I had gone with them, but I had to spend the day looking at the books in my office. Suddenly all the hands look off to the side of the house, where the trail comes from town.

I look and see about a rider coming up the trail to the house. As he gets closer, I recognize Lou from the Saloon. He rides up to the house and gets off his horse.

"Evening," I say, "how can I help you?" It's obvious from his expression that something is wrong.

"Henry," Lou says, "Kenedy is dead."

"What happened?" I ask, thinking I might already know.

"Two days back, he took a group of five deputies up to arrest Thompson, and none of them came back." Lou tells me, "so a couple of men went out that way yesterday and found Kenedy and all his deputies had been killed."

I hear the voice of Silas behind me, he has come up on us quietly and had apparently heard the news, "what about Thompson?"

"Gone," says Lou, "from what they could tell he left everything behind and hightailed it out of there. Just left his whole herd and ran."

"What now?" Silas asks.

"They have a posse going after him, but there's lots of places to hide in these mountains," Lou tells him.

"Sorry kid," I say, "at least it looks like you get your property back." I don't think this is much consolation to the kid; he's just looking at the ground.

"Yeah," he finally says quietly, "Ma will be glad we have something." I call Jesse over, I know he and Silas have been spending a lot of time working together. Jesse puts an arm around the boy.

"C'mon Silas," Jesse says, "let's get the horses ready to go over and round up your cattle."

"Ok," says the boy, "Pa would have wanted that." Silas and Jesse walk over to the stable and I walk up to the house. I should be relieved that this seems to rid us of Thompson, but I have a bad feeling that this isn't the end of our problems.

Once the horses are ready and we have a few extra men mounted up to help us round up the cattle we head out towards the pass that will take us to where I hope Thompson left the cattle. It's a quiet ride to the hidden valley, since Thompson was building there, it seemed the best place to start.

As we come through the narrow entrance to the valley, I can see the start of some corrals and a cabin close to the entrance. There are about forty head of cattle grazing quietly on the valley floor. I direct some of the men to start rounding them up. It will take a few men to take them back to our land and we can take up a search for the rest.

I know of a few good flats to keep cattle in these parts, but probably not all of them.
It is eerily quiet here, and as we look around the valley, we can see signs that this is where the fatal shootout with Kenedy must have happened. Flattened grass and a few empty shells here and there in the field.

Over by the half-built cabin we find signs of a camp, a fire pit and places where bedrolls were laid. I get off my horse and try to figure out how many people had made camp here. As I'm squatting down looking for some clue of what happened, I hear the loud retort of a gunshot echoing through the valley.

I'm up like a shot and looking around, to try and see what is going on. The cattle are spooked and the men are trying to calm them; Cody has his gun out and is looking into the hills. Jesse is riding around trying to help calm the cows. Silas is missing. His horse is riderless and moving around aimlessly.

Did he get off his horse? I look around trying to find him, I finally see a body lying on the ground close to his horse. As I am rushing over to him, I hear another shot and see one of my men fall off his horse.

"It came from over there!" yells Cody, pointing to a slope on the south side of the valley. The remaining cowboys are still trying to keep the cattle from running.

"Forget the cows!" I yell, "get some shelter." I watch the men move to sheltered areas and some of them dismount, all have their guns out and are looking around for more trouble. Cody has his rifle out and fires in the direction he thinks the shooter is. I rush over to Silas.

Silas is laying in the grass, gasping for air. He's alive. There is a lot of blood pumping from his shoulder, so when I get to him, I take my neckerchief and use it to try to stop the bleeding. A bullet slams into the ground near my foot, I didn't hear the shot, but now I can hear all kinds of shooting as my men are trying to find targets in the hills.

I spot a hollow under a fallen tree not far from us, so I drag Silas to the hollow and place him there. "He ok?" I hear Jesse next to me; he must have seen what was going on and came to help.

"I'm fine," I hear Silas grunt, "what's going on?"

"I don't think Thompson left," I say, drawing my gun and look around. As far as I can tell, I've lost one man and everyone else is hiding and looking about for targets.

"Who else is hit?" I ask Jesse, "did you see?"

"Looks like Bill," Jesse says. Bill Bolton had been with us for a long time. I look over at his body lying there and sigh. It's not moving at all, as I'm watching Kent rush over to him and pull him out of the sun into some shelter.

Jesse is tending to Silas' shoulder so I tell him to stay with him and rush over to where I can see Cody hunkered down by a bush.

"Can you see anyone?" I ask when I get to Cody.

"I'm not sure," he replies, "I think I hit someone on the southern slope, but it's hard to tell. No more shots have come from that spot."

"Ok," I say, "you get three men and try to get up that slope. Go slow." I figure there must be some men on that slope. "I'm going to go back to the pass and make sure they haven't closed that off. It would be best to get any wounded men out."

Cody sneaks over to where some of the other men are hidden and explains the plan to them before they get down low and move fast to the slope. The shooting has stopped, so I take a minute to figure out my route to the far end of the valley.

Once I have the most sheltered path figured out, I dash out from bush to tree. The odd shot rings out as I'm moving, but I'm too focused to try to think where they are coming from. I get to the entrance and hide low in some tall grass. I don't see any movement around, but I can see what looks like the heel of a boot sticking out from behind a rock big enough to hide a man.

I take careful aim and shoot the heel off the boot. I hear a man swear and see what looks like the top of a man's head, so I fire again. I hear a grunt and then see a man's head and shoulder appear, blood coming from his head. A flash comes from a bush to his left, I shoot in the direction of the flash, but I'm not sure if found my target or not.

I crawl up the slope and past the man I hit, heading for that bush. I get there to find a spot where a man was laying, but nobody is around. Quietly I move around the hill, but I don't find anyone else. I hear a few more shots echoing around the valley. I find a vantage point where I can get a better view of everything.

One of my men is down, probably dead and a few more are scattered around the valley floor. I can't see Jesse and Silas, but know they are hidden in that hollow. I see a man lying on the slope facing the valley. He fires in the direction of the fallen tree where Jesse is hiding. I see two flashes come from behind the fallen tree and watch the man jolt as a bullet tears through him. It looks like Silas is taking part in the fight, even though he is wounded. He's a tough kid.

Everything gets quiet and still. I hunker down in my spot and watch. It stays quiet for about twenty minutes, and I hear someone coming up behind me. I turn quickly, ready to fire but it's one of my men, James Smith, coming slowly down the slope.

"What's going on," I ask him quietly.

"I came around this way with Kent," he whispers, "we saw one man taking off back up the slope, but nothing else."

"Thanks," I say softly. I wonder if the man was retreating or getting to a better vantage point. I look across the notch in the slopes we use as an entrance and see Cody sneaking around a bush. He spots me and waves. He mimes that he too saw someone going up the slope. Maybe they had given up, seems weird to surrender when you have the high ground.

I slide down to the bottom of this slope and Cody disappears. When I get to the entrance, I see Cody coming towards me.

"I found one body," he says, "looks like he was in the spot I thought the first shots came from."

"So where did they all go?" I ask.

"From what I could tell there were only a few of them," he says.

"Thompson probably left a few men to watch over the cattle." I say thoughtfully. We walk back into the clearing, slowly looking around to see if we can see any sign of anyone. I want to be careful, but I also want to get Silas out of here.

I go to the hollow where Silas is laying and he looks rough. Jesse is watching the slopes. The remaining men saw me and all slowly made their way to me. When they had all taken position around us the men that had gone up the slope came across the valley floor.

"Alright boys," I say to them when they are all in earshot, "looks like they've taken off, is anyone else hurt?"

One of the men, Landon, nodded and growled out, "they grazed my left leg, it's not bleeding much though."

"I'm going to go around and round up as many horses as I can," I say, "let's get the wounded men up and out of here." I move around the valley quickly and gather up all the horses. Billy is lying dead, but the rest seem ok. The cattle are scattered all over the place but seem to be in good shape. A few brave men have come out to help me gather horses, but everything stays quiet.

We get Billy onto a horse and start getting Silas up on a horse. Since we are down one horse, and Silas looks very pale, Jesse jumps up behind Silas to ride with him back to the house. After we are all mounted it is obvious we have managed to scare off anyone left from Thomas' crew.

"Ok men," I say as we gather, "thank you for sticking with me. Cody, I'm going to ask you to help me round up these cows and get them back as fast as possible." As the others rode off Kent and Smith volunteered to stay behind and help.

Chapter 10

I have managed to get two women angry with me in one day. When Jesse rode up to the house with Silas, Jane and Emily took him into the house and started taking care of him. Jesse immediately took off to fetch the doctor. By the time I returned with the cattle, the doctor had the boy bandaged up and resting in Emily's room, being the only private room in the house.

This morning I'm sitting at the table drinking my coffee. Cody comes in and sits down next to me, he's been checking on our herd and the cows we brought in yesterday. He pours some coffee from the pot and leans back to enjoy it.

"How are things out there?" I ask.

"Fine," he says "the men are upset at losing Billy. They are talking about heading out there to find whoever's left and bringing them to justice."

"I'm trying to figure Thomas' plan," I say, "I think he left a small crew to watch the cattle so he can come back later to get them. Maybe get the posse on one trail then double back so they have more time to move them."

Emily enters with a stack of flapjacks; she hasn't said a word to me since I got back. She puts the dish on the table and then turns around and goes back into the kitchen sending me a death stare on the way.

"Sleeping in the kitchen doesn't seem to suit her," says Cody with a grin. We had put a cot in there since Silas has her bed.

"I'm thinking she's a bit too fond of that boy," I say.

"She couldn't do much better than him," says Cody, "Jesse tells me he didn't complain once yesterday, and even drew his gun and kept fighting."

"He's a tough kid alright," I respond thoughtfully. "I think we need to get up a group and go after Thompson." Like I said, revenge is a fool's game, but right now I'm feeling foolish. Thompson has pushed into my land, killed a man and stolen his cattle and now he has picked one fight too many with me.

"What are you thinking?" Cody says.

"Not sure yet," I say. I know I need a plan, but I just can't figure out what Thompson is thinking, if he is thinking. I know some men just respond to trouble without thinking of a plan. The fact he left some men behind makes me suspect he has some sort of plan.

Cody finishes his flapjacks and then stands up, “maybe we should get everyone together that wants to fight. Then come up with a plan.” Cody is proving that he has a good head on his shoulders, this is a good way to start. He goes out towards the bunkhouse.

As Cody is going out the door, Jane comes from the direction of Emily’s room. She pours herself a cup of coffee, which is not normal for her. She has been up all night caring for Silas.

“How’s the boy?” I ask.

“He’s lost a lot of blood,” she says sullenly, “the doctor said that if he makes it to the end of today, he should live.”

“I see,” I say quietly, “what do you think?”

“He’s strong and stubborn,” she says thoughtfully, “I think he’ll live.”

“That’s good news.” I say.

“I’m thinking of writing a letter to his Ma,” Jane says, “Silas says she can read.”

"Don't sent it until we have better news," I say, hoping to sound optimistic. "Cody and I getting a group of volunteers together to go after the rest of their property."

"And kill Thompson?" she knows how I think.

"Only if I have to," I say taking her hand, "I'm not as hellbent on revenge as I was when we first met."

"I'd hope you've matured a bit since then," she says with a smile.

"You've been a good influence," I tell her and then give her a gentle kiss. Jesse walks in, sees us and smiles. He pours himself the last of the coffee and gets the last of the flapjacks.

"Ma," he says between big bites, "how's Silas?"

"Sleeping right now," she says, "it's been a long night."

"Yeah," says Jesse, "I heard you moving around. You go rest, Ma, I'm ok to sit with him. Emily's around if I need any help." Jane looked at him with a smile.

"That's a good idea son," I tell him, "Jane you get some rest." Jane gets up and I stand with her. I escort her to our room and make sure she lays down. While she's getting settled, I grab a few things for the trail. I'm not expecting this is going to be a fast trip. I have no idea what to expect from Thompson. Before I leave, Jane is already fast asleep. I kiss her head softly and quietly leave the room.

I walk through to the kitchen where Emily is busy making bone broth. She doesn't look at me as I come into the room. I walk over to her and put a hand on her shoulder.

"Li'l bit?" I say, using the pet name I've had for her since she was little, "you know I had no way of knowing we were walking into an ambush." She stirs the broth slowly, staring into it and then sighs.

"Yeah Pa," she says "I know. Silas has been through a lot. It's hard to see him hurt."

"He's very brave," I say, "didn't let anything stop him from defending himself." Emily stops stirring and turns to me, her eyes watering up, she wraps her arms around me like she did when she was little. I hold her for a minute and let her cry and then step back, holding her at arm's length I look at her face.

"I need you to do something for me," I tell her. She nods so I continue, "please pack up some food for the trail, the whole team are going to look for the Lazy K cattle, Silas deserves to have his whole herd back." Emily smiles and wraps her arms around me again.

"Oh Pa!" she cries, "are you sure? That could be dangerous."

I give her a hug and tell her, "it'll be dangerous for anyone that tries to keep me from doing the right thing by that boy." She lets go of me and hugs me.

"Thanks Pa," she says, "now get out of the kitchen, I have work to do." As I leave, she moves around swiftly. It's always best to have a focus.

Chapter 11

It's been a week since we headed out to find Silas' herd. It has been slow going, and we have found about half of the herd. A steady stream of men taking cattle back to the ranch, bring back news that Silas is starting to sit up and is eating well. Jane sends word that she sent Jesse to town to mail a letter to his Ma, letting her know he is doing well.

We have left my land claim and are heading further out. There are currently eight of us on the trail, we are riding in a line, while we are still expecting trouble, there is some complacency as we figure Thompson must have moved on.

The sun is getting low and I'm thinking about finding a place to camp. Cody must be thinking the same as he rides up to me to discuss where we should camp. We spot a wide entrance to a cave and head over to look at it.

It is dry and looks big enough to fit the whole group. It is obvious that someone in the past has used it, there is some charred wood by the entrance. We decide this is a good place to spend the night and dismount.

After we stake the horses near some long grass and give them a brush down, Cody and Kent go off to find some good firewood. I get some food out of the saddle bags. The nice thing about having men going back and forth to the house is that we can have more fresh food. I eat some fresh cornbread and beans that Jane made for us. I transfer the beans from the jar Jane stored them in, into a pot. They smelled good cold.

Once the fire was going, we put the pot over it and got them heated up. Everyone ate their fill and leaned back to enjoy some coffee I had made. I get up to walk past the fire to the cave entrance when I hear a noise coming from the woods. I shush some of the men that are talking and listen again. There is something, or someone out there.

Our fire is set back a little in the cave, and we built it small since we don't really need it for heat. It is possible that someone walking by wouldn't even see it. The wood was dry and not giving much smoke, but there was still enough for someone to smell the fire. I go a little further into the trees and see some movement, someone is coming towards the cave.

I rush back into the cave to warn the men when I hear someone swear behind me. I turn to see the man that had been with Lassiter when he ambushed me. With him are three other men I don't recognize. I have my gun out as fast as I can manage and he does the same. I can hear many guns being cocked, we have a standoff.

"Gentlemen," I say cooly, "how are you this evening?"

Lassiter's pal looks at me and frowns, "what are you doing here?" he asks.

"Rounding up some stolen cattle." I reply.

"We didn't steal any of your cattle," said one of the other men.

"No," I reply, "but you drove a herd stolen out of Arizona to my land." The men all frown at me, thinking this through. I'm not sure if they are willing accomplices of this crime, or Thompson fooled them into thinking the Lazy K brand was his. "Can we just be reasonable?" I ask, "put our guns away and talk this out?"

The men look at each other and finally Lassiter's friend said, "this guy is a dead aim, he won't miss." The other men slowly lower their guns, and I indicate to my crew to do the same.

"I'm Henry Locke," I say, offering a hand to Lassiter's pal.

"Frank Shale," says the man, taking my hand, "this is Tommy Lots, Sam Doll and Will Porter." He indicates the other men. I take a closer look at Shale, he is about my height, dark complexion and has a scar on his left cheek. I invite the men to sit by the fire and offer them something to eat. Cody is looking at the men cautiously but doesn't say anything.

"How's Lassiter?" I ask.

"He was still alive last I saw him," says Shale, helping himself to some beans. "Says he'll come after you once he's better."

"Good to know," I say.

"He says you wouldn't have survived if his horse hadn't shied right before he fired" Shale continues, while eating the beans and cornbread.

I lean against the cave wall and take the man in, "he's probably right," I admit. The men eat their food and then Shale stands up and indicates to the others in the group to do the same. I see Cody's hand slowly move to his holster.

"Thanks for the grub" Shale says, "we should head out." The men brush themselves off and head out of the cave. We watch them go and then Cody walks over to the entrance of the cave.

"They rode off," he says after a minute, "so Thompson left more men behind."

"Yeah," I say, "or he turned back. But I don't see why he would split up the men if he did that." Thompson is a hard man to figure, I'm not sure what the best next step would be. One thing I am sure of, once a fool would sleep in this spot. "Men," I say decidedly, "let's break camp and head back home tonight."

" Good plan," says Cody. We start to break camp, but as I'm rolling my bedroll, I hear movement outside of the cave again. Cody hears it too and quietly indicates to the men to stop what they are doing.

I go to the mouth of the cave and look out, but don't see anything. Cody joins me, rifle in hand and looks around as well. He finally points in one direction, and I can see some branches moving slightly. It could have been something other than a man, but I don't want to take any chances.

"See if you can get to the horses," I whisper to Cody, "we might be able to sneak out of here if we walk them a bit." Cody nods and waves Kent over. He whispers the same directions to Kent and after Kent goes off, he turns to me.

"Kent was practically raised by Indians" he tells me, "man can sneak up on anything without being heard." I know where Kent is headed but can't see or hear the man. I'm glad he's on our side.

A minute of silence later Kent suddenly appears by my side. "They're gone," Kent tells me. "Someone cut the ropes." They are out there. I lay on the cave floor looking out but still can't see anything. I finally think of the start of a plan.

"Probably best to set up a fortress here," I whisper to Cody, let's get some rocks and wood and start a wall across the cave entrance. We quietly move some rocks and logs around to build a fortification that we can lay behind and rest rifles on. We decide to set up shifts, sleeping by our rifles so we can be better rested when trouble starts.

It's a long night, and even when it's my turn to sleep, I can't. My mind is racing to come up with a plan to get out of here. When I start to see the sun coming through the pine needles on the trees in have a plan.

I wave Cody and Kent over and tell them to leave their rifles and try to sneak out around behind whoever is out there. I'm pretty sure it's Shale and his crew, which means four men, but I can't be sure they didn't get reinforcements in the night. They hand their rifles to other men and head out quietly.

The sun is coming up quickly and the shapes out there are becoming bushes, felled trees and tree trunks. One of the shapes has also become the top of a man's head. At least that's what it looks like. If it is, he's not wearing a hat, it could be something else. I keep an eye on it, and suddenly I see it move and then disappear.

I'm sure it's a man, but don't really want to give away that we're on to them yet, so I keep an eye on the spot. As the sun gets higher, one of my men touches my shoulder and when I look, he hands me a cup of hot coffee. Someone had the initiative to get a fire going and get some breakfast cooking. I can smell some bacon cooking and smile. If there are men out there in ambush, they are having to smell the food cooking. I've been in a situation like that myself and know it is demoralizing. A plate of bacon and beans appears by my left elbow, and I eat while I watch for any movement.

It takes about an hour before anything happens. I see a hat off between two branches of a tree. It doesn't belong to Cody or Kent, and I'm getting a little impatient to see what's what. I aim for the very top of the hat and laugh when I see it fly off when I shoot at it. A voice in the woods swears.

Two guns fire in our direction from the woods, but both shots hit our little palisade. I hear another shot but don't see where it came from or lands. The men in the cave are on full alert now, watching the woods. I see some grass moving close to the cave. I wait until I can be sure it isn't Cody or Kent and then fire into the grass. There is a loud wail and then a bunch of bullets start flying at us.

We duck down low and I hear someone else cry out from the woods. I peek out and see a body running through the woods, so I take careful aim. I hear another shot and see him fall.

Everything goes quiet again. As far as I can tell there should be two more men out there. After a minute I hear Cody's voice.

"Hello camp," he shouts out, "all clear!" I stand up to see him standing out a way from the camp with Kent standing close by. He smiles and waves at us and I stand up and look around. Cody and Kent come back to the camp site and one of the men offers them each a plate of beans and bacon. It's cold, but they don't seem to care as they inhale the food.

"That one you shot that hat off was that Shale fellow," Cody says as he scrapes off the last of his beans, "he was the only one we hadn't tracked down, so when he swore I was able to shoot him. Kent used his knife on one of the men and one was shot from the cave, and I got the last guy as he was trying to run. We didn't see anyone else, so I guess we got them all."

While they rest a little, I take a group of men around to see if I can find out anything else. We can't see any sign of any other men, but we also can't find our horses. I look all over to try and find where Thompson's men left their horses but have no luck. I'm not sure what they could have done with them, and it's possible I will never find out. There are so many places to hide in these mountains that it's possible they won't be found. I've heard of horses managing to break free when desperate for water and I hope for their sakes they manage.

"It's a long walk home," Cody says with a concerned look on his face. I smile and agree with him. We discuss staying at the cave for one more night and then heading out the next morning. Since we have our gear with us, we at least have enough food for a while longer.

Chapter 12

I've never been one for walking, we've been going since first light and now it's getting close to noon. I'm hot and thirsty and getting a little grouchy. All the men are, so it's become a sullen walk. Since we aren't sure if any more Thompson's men are around, we decided to Kent suddenly stops and his had goes to his gun.

"Riders coming," he says quietly. I stop and listen and I can hear a lot of riders. We get off the trail and find a good place to stash our gear and then try to get some cover. I quickly tell half the men to go on one side of the trail while I take position with Cody and Kent.

It is a long, tense minute before I see the riders off in the distance. I have my rifle trained on them and am ready for a fight. As they get closer, I recognize some of the horses. I recognize them because I've ridden most of them. It's my men, being led by Jesse. Cody recognizes this at about the same time, and we jump up to make sure the men don't open fire.

Jesse comes up with all the men we left at the ranch. As soon as he sees me, he stops his horse and jumps off.

"Pa!" he says excitedly, "we thought you were dead." I smile at him and walk over to him, taking him by the hand.

"Dead tired," I say, "and glad to see you." Cody comes over and claps Jesse on the back.

"What are you doing out here?" Cody asks.

"Your horses came back early this morning," Jesse explains. "We mounted up and came running as soon as we saw them."

"Glad you did," I say cheerfully, "my feet are rubbed raw." We discuss who will share a horse, so nobody has to walk. We mount up and head home.

When we get to the ranch house, the sun is very low in the sky. We take the horses into the stable and Jesse and some of the men offer to brush them down so I can rest. The horses that had made it home before us had been treated well by Emily, all cleaned up and fed and watered.

I walk over to the house and Emily rushes out and throws her arms around me. "Pa!" she cries out. This brings Jane out, and she is a bit more reserved, but obviously she has been very worried about me. After Emily finally releases me, I give Jane a hug and kiss her before we go into the house.

When we get into the house, I see Silas sitting on the settee in the sitting room. He's still a little pale but looking a little better.

"Mr. Locke," he says, trying to stand. I indicate that he should stay seated and walk over and sit in the high back chair next to him.

"How are you lad?" I ask.

"Better," he says, "The doctor says everything is mending up good." I'm glad to hear it and let him know. Jane has gone into the kitchen and comes out with a plate of food for me and puts it on the table. I go over to a cabinet and pull out a bottle of whiskey and pour myself some. It is good to be home.

After I've eaten and am feeling more relaxed, I go to the pump behind the kitchen and wash the dust from the last week off as best I can. I go to my room and find that Jane has already laid out some clean clothes for me.

Refreshed and fed now, I head out to the stable. Jesse and Cody are out there; Cody is telling Jesse about the last few days. I walk over to them and they turn to me.

"Sounds like I missed out," Jesse says with a smile.

"Yeah, missed a long walk," I say, "how are things here."

"Good," Jesse says, "a few of us managed to get some fencing up at the Hidden Valley. That's where we're keeping Silas' herd."

"Good plan," I say, glad he took the initiative. I walk around the stable, looking in on Little Red who's looking much better. It's been a hard couple of weeks around here.

The sun is down as I walk back to the house. The air is cool and I'm starting to feel the stress of the last twenty-four hours fall off me. When I was younger, I lived for this type of thing, but having settled down and gotten comfortable with a roof over my head and steady meals now felt like the better way to live.

As I reach the house, Jane is sitting on the bench on our front porch. I walk over to her and sit down. "How are you doing?" I ask her.

"It's been a long week," she says quietly, "I've been worried about you all week, and then when your horse came home without you…" her voice breaks and I realize she is starting to cry. I put my arm around her and apologize for all the trouble we've been dealing with.

"It's not your fault," she says with a sniff, "and I'm glad were able to help Silas and his Mom. She raised him right; he's been trying not to be a burden on us as he heals."

"Really?" I ask, "that's good."

"You know that Emily is taken with him?" she says Jane, sounding a bit wistful.

"I've suspected that" I say quietly, "not sure I'm ready for that. But I do suppose it shows I can trust her taste in men."

"Of course you can," she says, "she wants a man like her Pa." Jane puts a hand on my knee and lays her head on my shoulder. I wrap my arm around her shoulder and we sit quietly, enjoying the time together.

Chapter 13

"You slept in," says Jesse as I walk into the dining room. I look at the tall clock in the sitting room and smile. It's half past eight in the morning, so I did sleep an extra hour and a half. I never sleep in, so I suppose it's cause for comment.

"I think I've earned a sleep in," I say, "don't you?" We sit down and Jane enters from outside.

"Henry," she's said with some alarm, "Cody needs to see you." I get up and rush outside to see Cody is saddling two horses. I rush over to him; he sees me coming and turns to look at me.

"Pa," he says, "we've just gotten word from the Hidden Valley." He sinches up the saddle on the second horse and turns to me again. "Thompson is up there with at least twenty men; they are rounding up the cattle to get them out of there."

I rush back to the house to get my guns and by the time I'm back outside and see every able bodies man on my ranch is saddled up and loaded for bear. I mount my horse and look at all of them.

"Men," I say, "Thompson isn't going to give up easily. This is going to be a hard ride and a tough fight. You are all good men and loyal, anyone that doesn't feel up to this fight, I will not resent anyone who turns back."

"We'll follow you to hell, if need be," says Kent, and all the men agree. I hear a few of them mention poor Bill. We take off, riding hard for the hidden valley. At this pace we should be able to make the valley in about an hour.

The ride is hard and dusty, and we get to Morrison's pass in record time. We slow down a bit as we get closer to the valley. We take our horses off the trail as we get closer to the valley entrance so they can't see us coming. We can hear the noise r the cowboys urging the cows along the trail. As we get closer, we stop and start to talk strategy.

I have a plan, but my boys aren't too fond of it. I ride around to the trail where I can see Thompson's men directing the cattle down the trail. I put my horse ahead of them in the middle of the trail.

"Thompson you there?" I yell out. Everyone stops and looks at me. After a still moment, the only sound behind the sound of the cattle complaining about being moved out and then suddenly stopped, I see Thompson ride through the entrance, riding through the cattle to get to me.

"Locke," he says with disdain, "what do you want?"

"You're stealing cattle from a friend of mine," I tell him.

"You've got no right," he starts, but I interrupt him quickly.

"I have every right," I tell him, "I have proof of ownership of these cows and they are on my land."

"It's all mine by right of possession," he yells out.

"That's not in the law and you know it," I say carefully. Thompson glares at me and I can see he has settled one hand close to his gun. My heart starts to race and my muscles tense as I know this is going to end with one of us dead. My boys know to let things play out, and hopefully the talking works.

"He didn't steal nothing!" says one of the men riding for Thompson. I've never seen him before, I look around and realize I've not seen any of these men.

"Got some new men riding for you I see." I say, looking around.

"You killed all my other men." Thompson growls.

"I'll kill them too if they fight me," I threaten. I look at the men, "men, the man you're riding for is a murderer and a theif!"

"Who cares!" yelled one man. I look at him, he's a rough looking man carrying two pistols and has a rifle resting on the pommel of his saddle. I recognize a hired gun when I see one. In fact they all look like they were hired to fight.

"I see you came expecting a fight" I say to Thompson.

"You don't seem the quitting sort," he said, "I knew you'd come to steal my cows." I would argue that again but realize that I'm not going to win any of these men. His horse takes a step back and he reaches for his gun.

Not being the fastest draw I've learned a few tricks to beat a fast draw. I get my horse to step to the side while I palm my colt. I have a bead on him and fire at the same time as he does. His shot goes to where I was and mine hits him in the side.

He falters for a second and sits up again, taking aim. I cock my colt and bring it up firing into his head. His head whips back as the shot hits it, his gun firing again as he falls off the horse, the round flying harmlessly into a tree.

My horse is well trained, and is normally hard to upset, but this has been too much action and he's circling a bit to show he's upset. I grab the reins to get control, keeping an eye on Thompson's men.

I see Lassiter up the trail, looking pale. His expression is one of shock as he sees his boss hit the ground. I get to see the famed fast draw one time before I see a flash on my right side, and he crumples and falls off his horse. I turn to see Silas; in all this excitement I didn't even realize he had joined the group. His gun is in his hand, and he has a determined look on his face.

I look around and see that most or Thompson's men are looking on in shock. Their boss and the famous Tom Lassiter are lying dead, and it's been less than a minute.

There is a quick flurry of movement as they come to their senses and draw to fight their way out of there. My men all ride out of the woods; guns trained on the gunslingers.

"It isn't worth your life," I say to Thompson's men. "Your boss is dead and isn't paying wages. But I'll pay a day's wages for any man that helps get these cattle back into the valley." This encourages most of them to put their guns away and start the work of turning the cattle around. My men start helping as well. A few men decide to ride off, which saved me some money.

Jesse and Silas ride down to my side, "good shooting kid," I say, "it's a hard thing to take a man's life, but I appreciate the back-up."

"I can't believe he's dead," Silas says, looking down at Thomson's body. He's been on the revenge trail for a while, it's always a bit of a letdown when it ends.

"Revenge is never quite what you think it will be," I say to him, "but now we can get these cattle back to your ranch and you and your Ma should do Ok."

Epilogue

Winter is just around the corner, but the weather is still holding out. I look at Cody and Jesse as they finish getting their gear packed up for the trail. We've spent a few weeks finding as many of the Lazy K cattle as we can. We have almost all the cattle that Thompson stole from the Trent ranch. We talked it over and decided that there should be enough time to drive the cattle back to Silas' land.

Emily has been sulking ever since the decision was made for Silas to head home. I guess losing your first love is hard, but she's still helping get things ready for the drive. She's even spent some time making a fantastic farewell meal for the boys.

As they are mounting up, Silas comes to me looking as healthy as the day he showed up at our door. "Mr. Locke," he says offering his hand. I take it and shake, "thanks for all you've done."

"It's no problem," I say to him, "take care on the drive home. You be sure to write and let us know how it goes."

"Yes sir," he pauses for a moment, looking over at the house where Jane and Emily are standing, having already said their goodbyes. "And sir?" he asks, "I know we're still young and all, but I expect in a year or two I'll come calling." I look at him for a second in confusion.

"Calling?" I ask.

"Yes sir," he says seriously, "I expect Emily is going to be real hard to forget." He turns quickly, his face turning red and rushes back to get on his horse. I watch him go for a second in disbelief.

"Silas," I call after him, "that would be fine by me." He looks at me and waves back, a huge smile on his face. I walk up to the house and stand between Jane and Emily, my arms around each one. Jane gives me a funny look and I smile at her.

Author's note:

This book is the prequel to a series telling the exploits of the gunslinger Silas Trent. Later to be known as Short Hand Trent.

The following is an excerpt from the first book of the series "Silas' Trail"

Silas Trent was still hurting as he sat astride the horse, a paint with boots, and looked at his worst enemy who was talking. Henry Locke was distracting him by talking, he could shoot him now. Silas drew his gun, staring down the sight at Jack Thompson. He could see the arrogant look on his face as he dared to suggest he was the rightful owner of the Lazy K. Silas was the rightful owner, he could shoot him right now. He watched Thompson reach for his gun.

Shoot!

Why couldn't he shoot? He should shoot. He was here to avenge his father by killing this man. Thompson drew his gun and fired at Henry Locke, the man that helped him hunt Thompson.

Shoot!

Thompson almost fell out of his saddle; his side was bleeding. Silas wondered if he had shot. No. Locke had shot, but hadn't killed him. Now was his chance. Silas heard the shot and watched Thompson's head whip back as Locke shot him between the eyes. Out of the corner of his eyes, Silas saw a blur. He turned and fired. It was easier when he didn't think. He saw a man slump and fall off his horse. He had killed a man. He looked over at Locke, the man who had been about to shoot the man that avenged his father's death, surely he had done the right thing.

The world started spinning. Everything was a blur. He could see his dead father lying on the ground. He could see Matt bleeding out onto the parched soil. Spinning again, brown and green, spinning. He saw his mother, weeping, holding Matt's hand. But no. It wasn't his mother, it was the mother of the man lying dead. The mother of the man he killed. Weeping.

Silas jumped up, it was a nightmare. He looked around the campfire at his companions all sleeping soundly on the ground. The night air was cold so Silas laid back down and wrapped himself in his blanket. The nightmare had become a regular thing for him. He lay there thinking about all the events that lead to him killing Tom Lassiter. Silas had been after Lassiter's boss, Jack Thompson, a cattle thief who had killed his father. Silas had teamed up with the Locke family up in Colorado to find Thompson and his fathers cattle, now his cattle. They had also sent their two sons Cody and Jesse to help him drive the cattle back to his home in Arizona.

They were over a week into the drive home and were camped out in a valley between two ragged peaks. Silas could just make out the outline of them in the night sky. While he personally loved the wider spaces where he grew up, he had to admit the mountains of Colorado were a beautiful place to visit. Silas heard one of his partners moving around, he looked over to see Tobias Kent, one of the men sent with him to help drive the cattle. He could tell that Tobias was looking at him in the dark and slowly moved over in his direction.

"You alright kid?" Tobias whispered once he got close enough. Even though Silas was technically the owner of the drive, all the men were being paid by the Locke family. At fifteen years old, Silas was the youngest in the group. Everyone treated him like an equal most of the time, he worked as hard as everyone, but at camp he still became "kid." It didn't really bother him, since it was a term of fondness and not making fun.

"Bad dream." said Silas.

"Been there" Tobias sighed, "I try to think of something nice."

"Like what?" Silas asked.

"Me? I think of a dancing girl in the saloon back at Victor. Her legs make a man quiver." Tobias looked over at Silas and grinned, "mebbe you're still a bit young for that." Tobias inched back to his bedroll and looked up into the sky, his hands behind his head. Silas was sure he was grinning up at the sky thinking about those legs. Silas rolled onto his side and thought his own good thoughts. Back on the Locke ranch there was a girl, Emily. She was the most beautiful girl he has ever seen, she had blonde hair that looked like spun gold and a smile that made him feel warm inside. As he was thinking thoughts about her, he drifted back off to sleep.

The next morning as they were breaking camp, Cody came over to Silas. He put a hand on the younger man's shoulder and smiled. Cody was over a foot taller than Silas' four foot ten and had dark hair. Silas had long blond hair himself, he didn't much like anyone touching it, so going to the barber wasn't a priority.

"Once we get over the last range, we should be crossing into New Mexico," Cody said, "maybe take us about two days unless something goes wrong."

James Smith, the other man sent along to help, looked up at Cody quickly. “Don’t tempt fate,” he said with a scowl.

Cody laughed and turned to James, “I don’t believe in that nonsense,” he said. James glared at him but said nothing. Silas could hear him muttering to himself as he rolled up his bedroll and started to get his gear onto his horse.

Silas packed his own gear onto his horse, a paint that Emily had lovingly named Boots. This horse was on loan until he made it out of the mountains, and he could start riding his pony again. He felt sorry for his pony, being used as a pack horse, but it was too uncertain on these rocky slopes to be trusted with a rider.

The men all started the task of getting the cattle moving down the slopes. It was tedious work for the most part, making sure the cows stayed on the trail and didn’t wander off. Even though a winter chill was starting to fill the air, it wasn’t long before Silas had shrugged his long coat off his shoulders. The men moved amongst the herd prodding on stragglers and making sure none of the cows strayed. While it was a team task, each man was left to their own thoughts. Silas daydreamed about Emily most of the time, some of his thoughts were probably best to keep from her brothers who were riding nearby. Sometimes, though, he thought about his Ma.

Silas had been there when his father and brother were murdered, he had caught a bullet in his side in the fight. His memory of how he got back home was a little vague. He remembers someone finding him and putting him on a horse, but the particulars weren't there. His Ma said it was Jedediah Boone, a rancher who lived close to them, that saved him. After recovering from his wounds, Silas had decided to go after the man that killed his father. His Ma didn't like that idea and told him not to go. After a few weeks of struggling with constant visions of revenge, Silas decided he absolutely had to get his revenge and snuck out of the house one night when everyone was asleep.

He wasn't sure what his Ma would say when he returned. Mrs. Locke had written a letter to let her know he was ok, but that was a while back. He knew she was probably worried about him, but it was also good to be bringing back the herd that had been stolen. It wasn't much, a few hundred head, but Silas was confident he could manage them and help him, and his Ma survive.

They came up to a narrow pass between two steep slopes and directed the lead cows toward it, knowing the rest would follow fairly easily. Tobias was in the lead, and it wasn't long before Silas couldn't see him as the pass took a turn downhill. Jesse was a ways ahead of him as they had the cows moving in twos and threes through the pass. Cody was behind, with James riding drag at the rear to encourage stragglers.

Suddenly Cody swore and yelled out "rock slide!" Silas looked up and saw rocks tumbling down the slope to the left. Some smaller rocks flew through the air and hit a couple of the cows ahead of Silas, they cried out in pain. This started to make the other cows nervous. While they needed to move fast, they also needed to keep them from stampeding. Silas urged Boots on ahead and tried to get the cattle around him to pick up the pace.

Some of the younger cows were trying to turn and get away from the danger while the older ones seemed to trust the cowboy's urging. More rocks fell and Silas saw a large boulder hit one heifer on head. He heard a sickening crack as her skull caved, she slumped to the side and was caught up in the rush of bodies for a second before being sucked underfoot and was trampled. Silas tried to keep one eye on the herd and one on the rocks.

He heard Jesse grunt as a smaller rock hit him. “You hurt?” Cody yelled across at him.

“Hit my arm,” yells Jesse, “I’m not sure it isn’t broken.” Cody swore again as he pushed closer to his brother. Jesse waved him off, “just get through this, I’ll be ok.”

Silas breathed a sigh of relief as he saw an opening ahead, letting out into a wide space. As he urged the cattle through it he looked back. From the looks of it the rock slide had slowed down. As the last of the herd came down into the valley floor they had entered. James brought the last of them into the valley and the men all worked to stop the cattle moving. There was a spring over to the right side of the valley feeding into a pond, and the cows all wandered over to get something to drink.

As soon as things looked settled Cody rushed over to his brother. Jesse was cradling his left arm in his right and looked a little pale. Cody got off his horse and helped Jesse down and took a close look at the arm. It was bruised and starting to swell.

“How does it feel?” Cody asked.

"I'm pretty sure it's broken," Jesse said through gritted teeth. Tobias rode over to them and got off his horse. Tobias went to his saddlebag and took a kerchief out and looked around for two straight branches about the same length. He walked back over to Jesse and looked at his arm.

"Looks broke to me," he told Jesse, "I kin splint it, but that'll hurt. Mebbe best to get a swig of whiskey." James rode over and pulled a whiskey bottle out of his saddle bag. Cody gave him a look, the Locke family had a policy against drinking on a drive.

James saw the look and shrugged, "good thing I brought it," he said. He handed it down to Tobias who tipped the bottle up to Jesse's lips. Jesse took a swallow and coughed little. Tobias straighted Jesse's arm and the look on Jesse's face showed the Whiskey wasn't doing much to help. Tobias lined up the branches and expertly tied them on with the kerchief from his bag and the one he had tied around his neck.

The sun was still high in the sky, but the men all decided it was time to set up camp to let Jesse rest. Cody got Jesse's bedroll off his horse and got him situated, sitting against a fallen tree. Silas staked the horses and spent some time getting their saddles off and rubbing them down. The horses seemed to appreciate an early quitting time, chomping on the long grass in the valley. James rode over to the herd to keep watch over them and keep them from wandering off. It was a bit early to bed them down, but with fresh water and lush grass they weren't likely to wander far.

Tobias started to collect firewood and build a fire. Once he had some good coals going, he started making coffee. Silas walked over to the cows and started to do a quick check over of them to see if any were badly injured. James rode over to him.

"From what I can see three were trampled," James told Silas, "I can see a few that are bleeding, I've been trying to corral them together over there." James pointed over to a spot where some bushes made a natural coral and about five or six cows were standing. "I warned you this morning," he said, "you don't tempt fate."

www.ingramcontent.com/pod-product-compliance
Lightning Source LLC
Chambersburg PA
CBHW021327060726
47591CB00006B/1912

* 9 7 8 1 9 7 2 8 0 3 1 2 7 *